Presented to

ANNE CRAIG

FOR

PERFECT

ATTENDANCE

1975/76

PICKERING & INGLIS LTD.   PRINTED IN GREAT BRITAIN

D0532528

Other titles by Diana Pullein-Thompson
in the Armada series include

Janet Must Ride
A Pony for Sale
I Wanted a Pony
The Hermit's Horse

Horses at Home and *Friends Must Part* were first published in
the U.K. in 1954 by Wm. Collins Sons & Co. Ltd., London
and Glasgow.
This edition was first published in 1969 by May Fair Books Ltd.,
14 St. James's Place, London SW1A 1PF.

© Diana Pullein-Thompson 1954

Printed in Great Britain by
Love & Malcomson Ltd.,
Brighton Road, Redhill, Surrey.

HORSES AT HOME

and

Friends must part

DIANA PULLEIN-THOMPSON

Armada

ILLUSTRATIONS

CHAPTER ONE

NICHOLAS AND I like Auntie Gay best of all our relations. She isn't like a real aunt; she is young and brave and dashing; she hunts and she jumps in international competitions, and she has two famous horses, called Jubilee and Harvester.

She forgets our birthdays sometimes and she only gives us very small presents at Christmas, compared with the pound notes Auntie Jane and Auntie Carol send us, and she can be very downright and snubbing; but she is the only person who is really interested in our riding and she is always trying to persuade our parents to buy us ponies.

We love going to tea with Auntie Gay and sometimes she lets us ride Harvester and Jubilee. She lives alone in a cottage with her springer spaniel and Siamese cat. She is always broke, but she seems to get more fun and excitement out of life than most people. Mummy says that Auntie Gay has a single-track mind and if we have ponies we'll have single-track minds too, but Nicholas and I don't think that is true and we feel a dreadful pull at our heart-strings each time we look at the two loose-boxes at the end of our garden.

As Nicholas says, it would be different if our parents couldn't afford to buy us ponies, but they can. They spend a small fortune on dull things like school uniforms and visits to the British Museum and the Tower of London, and now they've built us a playhouse in the garden, which must have cost at least a hundred pounds.

In books children who want ponies get them by putting out fires or saving lives or catching thieves, and often I lie in bed willing something like that to happen to me, but it never does.

But we are luckier than many children, because we have riding lessons at the local riding school and, though most of the ponies seem very tired and Auntie Gay disapproves of the instruction we are given, it is lovely to ride at all.

The riding school is owned by Captain Pike, who has clean-cut features and pale blue eyes, but he spends most of his time buying and selling horses and he leaves a girl, called Pauline, to give the riding lessons. Nicholas *hates* Pauline and, whatever she says, he obstinately follows Auntie Gay's method and style of riding. I try to compromise and end by pleasing nobody. I don't think Pauline is *so* awful and she works very hard, but in a way she is a fright and I suppose all boys hate frights. Anyway, she orders Nicholas around in rather a bossy tone of voice and he takes as little notice as possible, which can be very embarrassing for me. She has short mouse-coloured hair, cut like a boy's, a large nose and a loud harsh voice, and she's rather fat. Nicholas swears all the ponies at the riding school hate her, but I don't think this is true.

I am sure Pauline disapproved very much of what happened at the beginning of the Easter holidays, which is when this story begins.

Nicholas and I broke up on the same day and we were both glad to be home, especially as Auntie Gay had invited us to tea the very next day. We looked at our tortoises, which were still hibernating, and kissed our mongrel dog. Gambler, and our parents' pedigree poodle, Chiffon, and talked endlessly of school. We were sitting in the stable and admiring the two loose-boxes when Mummy came running down the gravel path to the garage. Mummy doesn't run very often and the sight surprised us.

"What's up?" called Nicholas. "Anything wrong?" She stopped.

"It's Gay. She's been rushed to hospital in an ambulance with appendicitis. I'm going there at once," said Mummy, slipping into the car.

"Auntie Gay—ill? Oh, how awful! But what's happened to the horses and Luke and Picaroon? There'se nobody to give them their tea," I cried.

"Humans come before animals. I'll ring up Daddy later on and tell him how she is—when he gets back," said Mummy, starting the engine.

"Is it a matter of life and death, then? Is she seriously ill?" demanded Nicholas, leaping on to the running-board.

My heart jumped and I felt a sinking in the pit of my tummy.

"No. Get off, Nicholas. I've told you; it's appendicitis. You know what that is. Now be good, both of you, and tell Daddy I'll be ringing him."

"But why the hurry?" called Nicholas desperately as the car slid away down the drive.

"It's no good. She won't explain. Poor Auntie Gay. How awful to be ill all alone," I said.

"Well, if it is just appendicitis there's nothing to worry about—plenty of people have that. But I think it's something worse," said Nicholas gloomily. "Mummy wouldn't be tearing around like that unless it was something pretty urgent."

"I'm worried about the horses. I bet nobody has given them a thought," I said.

Nicholas consulted his watch. "It's only half-past three. We've got time to bike over there. We can leave a written message for Daddy," he suggested.

7

"But won't Mummy be furious when she finds out?" I wondered.

When Nicholas makes a decision he sticks to it through thick and thin. He said:

"It is our duty to Auntie Gay to see that her animals are looked after all right. We can ring up the cottage and if there is no reply we must investigate. I'll go and telephone now. But it's not as though she even had a charlady."

I was going to hear a lot about our duty to Auntie Gay from Nicholas in the next few weeks, though I didn't know that now.

Ten minutes later we were biking down the road, silent and anxious. There had been no reply from Cherry Tree Cottage and our minds were with Auntie Gay in Flaxborough Hospital. I wished we knew more. Who had telephoned Mummy and was the operation over when they rang? Who found Auntie Gay or had she called in the doctor herself? Nicholas and I both knew all too well that she hated calling in doctors; she never believed she was ill, and once she walked and rode for a fortnight with a broken collar-bone. It was Daddy, her brother, who finally insisted that she should have it X-rayed. No, I guessed she had been found by the baker lying prostrate in her cottage.

The wind was against us and, in spite of this, Nicholas bicycled fearfully fast and left me yards away. If I hadn't been worried I should have been very angry; my legs ached and my eyes watered and I prayed he would not keep up the same speed all the way, the eight miles, to Cherry Tree Cottage.

"What's up with Stephen?" he called suddenly.

Stephen is the name I have given my bike. I don't like him; he kicks my shins when I kindly lead him up the hills and he has slow punctures and pinches my fingers when I try to mend them, so I have given him

8

the name I dislike most of all Christian names. Nicholas's bike is called The Black Demon.

"He's stiff and lazy," I yelled back. I always blame Stephen on these occasions, never myself.

"Bad luck! I'll wait. Demon's a dream. He knows it's urgent—telepathy." Nicholas always pretends to believe my excuses about Stephen. I suppose it gives him a sense of superiority to find he is so much faster than me on a bike and that makes him feel strong and kind.

He waited. Then he said, "Hold on to my hand. I'll give you a pull." I felt I was being rather feeble, but my legs were aching so I accepted.

Evening was in the air when we reached Cherry Tree Cottage. The garden gate stood wide open and we could see Picaroon looking out of the window; there was something very forlorn about it and rather frightening. We threw our bikes in the ditch and ran to the front door, which was locked. Then we tried the back, got in, and let out poor Picaroon, who was delighted to see us. He ran round and round in circles, but Luke stayed firmly on the kitchen chimney-piece. We visited the horses next and Jubilee welcomed us with a whinney.

"Nobody has been here, you see," said Nicholas. "They've just been abandoned. Poor old Harvester! Never mind. We'll look after you." He patted the liver chestnut's sleek neck as he spoke. I ran to Jubilee and she licked my hands and searched my pockets.

"How wonderful to have the smell of hay and horses after musty old school! Jubilee, my darling, Auntie Gay is ill; she's been taken to hospital, but she'll be all right soon," I explained.

We cleaned out the stables and fetched fresh hay and water, and then we gave each horse a feed of oats and chaff, and changed their buff and red day rugs for jute night rugs. We had rather a job, because Jubilee is fifteen hands and Harvester is sixteen hands, and Nicholas and I are not tall for our ages. But at last we had settled them for the night and we turned our attention to the other animals.

"We can't leave Picaroon and Luke here alone all night. It just isn't fair," decided Nicholas.

"They will be dreadfully worried," I added, looking at the spaniel's mournful eyes.

"They must come home with us—that's definite," said Nicholas firmly.

"I hope Daddy won't be furious. Chiffon will hate Picaroon," I muttered.

"It's our duty to Auntie Gay to look after her animals. I shall stay here the night if Daddy complains," said Nicholas.

"I'm sure he won't," I said hastily.

"Well, look, can you carry Luke on your bike?— he's very light—and I'll lead Picaroon from mine."

"Okay, but we better leave a note saying we've taken them, in case anyone turns up to look after them," I suggested.

Stephen did not like taking Luke very much and wobbled furiously, but The Black Demon and Picaroon went beautifully together and Nicholas called back—he was well ahead of me—that we had better swop halfway. Luke miaowed pitifully and struggled under my arm, and I felt sure Auntie Gay would be very angry if she saw her cat being treated in this way. I tried to explain the situation to him as we had explained it to the horses, but he would not listen and his miaows nearly drowned my words.

Then an awful thing happened; we were turning a corner, close to a wood, when Luke gave a wrench and a twist and leapt from my arms. I braked and swerved, and then Stephen and I went diving into the

10

ditch. Stephen, of course, landed on top of me in his usual thoughtless manner and I had to push him back before I could struggle to my feet, and his chain came off. I couldn't see Luke *anywhere*, and when I called his name no miaows answered me. Nicholas hadn't noticed and was already round the next corner and out of sight.

I started to search the edge of the wood. Unfortunately there was a good deal of undergrowth and last year's bracken matched Luke's coat, so he could not have chosen a better place to hide.

I called his name over and over again, and presently Nicholas came back and said, "You don't mean to say you've let him go? Oh, Clare!"

Dusk had fallen and the wood was very quiet and you could hear every rustle amongst the old brown bracken and the last leaves of autumn. I investigated scores of rustles but not one was Luke. Now and again I saw a little mound of earth or a piece of weed or just a dark patch, a shadow cast by the branches of a tree, and I thought they were Luke and my heart leaped with joy, only to be disappointed a moment later.

"Picaroon might find him," suggested Nicholas. "Come on, Picaroon, find Luke—Luke! Search for him, search!"

But Picaroon only went off in full cry after a rabbit.

"You know, it will be dark soon. And our parents will be in a fearful flap. How on earth did he escape from you?" asked Nicholas.

I explained and then he said, "Well, look, you had better go home and tell Daddy what's happened and I'll stay and search for Luke."

"Oh, I couldn't do that," I said firmly. "I lost him and I must find him—whether I have to stay out all night. You go home and tell them and I'll stay. It's all my fault."

"Don't be silly. Everybody knows cats are jolly slippery things to hold. We were both to blame. We ought to have thought of putting him in a hamper," said Nicholas.

I started to crawl on my hands and knees, because I hoped I would see under the bracken better this way. A car slid by on the road and its lights lit up the wood for a moment.

"Look, Clare, I think you really ought to go home and tell our parents. They'll be dreadfully worried, especially when they remember Stephen hasn't any lights. It will be dark soon," said Nicholas.

"The Black Demon hasn't any lights either. Oh, I do wish I could find Luke! I feel so awful and he must be so frightened. Luke, Luke, pussy pussy!" I called.

"I know I haven't any lights either, but dash it all, I'm a boy and I'm two years older than you. It's obvious if one of us must stay out it should be me. When you get home you can organise a proper search party with a car. It's quite different a boy of fourteen being out alone in the dark with a bike without lights from a girl of twelve," said Nicholas.

"But, Nicholas, I can't bike back anyway, because Stephen has let me down as usual. His chain's off."

But my brother was not to be put off so easily.

"We'll soon put that right," he said. "You catch Picaroon and put his lead on and I'll deal with Stephen."

Nicholas won the day, and presently I was biking sadly homewards. Never had five miles seemed so long and never had I felt so dreary. We had wanted to help Auntie Gay so badly and all we had done was to make matters worse by losing poor little Luke. It would have been different, I reflected, if he had been an ordinary cat, able to kill a rabbit for himself and glad to spend a night out in the woods. But, although Auntie Gay does not spoil her animals, he had been brought up to look to humans to provide him with everything; and now we had let him down.

I reached home in a state of gloom and found Mrs. Tubb, who comes in daily to help with the cooking, in the kitchen.

"Clare, where 'ave you been? I've been worried to death. And where's Nicholas? What on earth's happened? You are not crying?" she said.

"Oh, Tubb! We've lost Luke. Nicholas is still looking. Auntie Gay's in hospital. Where's Daddy? I had to lead Stephen the last mile. It's so dark," my words came out in a rush and I was near tears.

Mrs. Tubb tried to be soothing. "Now, sit down, duck, and calm yourself. Your father has gone to be with your aunt. She's seriously ill—something itis, they say she's got. I forget the name. But your mummy and daddy are going to spend the night in Flaxborough, so they can be within call, and they've asked me to sleep 'ere, to look after you and Nick. And when I comes, bless me if neither of you is 'ere. Worried to death, I've been."

"Tubb, is she going to die?" I asked, and I waited terrified lest she should say yes.

"Well, they say it's serious, very serious, but I reckon she'll be all right. There're some very clever doctors at Flaxborough, very clever, they say. Don't you worry, duck; worrying won't do anybody any good, will it?"

"But she might die?" I persisted.

"Yes, but I don't reckon it's likely, that I don't. Your aunt 'as always been a very strong woman. She'll pull through—you see if she don't."

"We've lost Luke," I said, in tragic accents. "And Nicholas has no lights on The Black Demon."

"And who in the world is Luke?" asked Mrs. Tubb.

13

Then I told her my sad story. "What shall we do now?" I finished.

She was silent for a moment—and it is not often Mrs. Tubb is lost for words.

"I wish your father was here," she said after a while, and it seemed such a silly useless wish that I felt almost annoyed for a minute. After all she was a grown-up—surely she could help.

"I've got it!" she exclaimed suddenly. "You stay 'ere like a good girl. Now don't get into any more mischief. And I'll pop 'ome and 'ave a word with Bert. 'E's got young Sid Middleton coming up to-night with 'is motor-bike. Sid could go down and fetch Nick."

"Oh, Tubb, you're marvellous!" I cried. "Nicholas will love going on the back of the motor-bike. I do hope he's found Luke."

"All right. I'll pop along now. Remember what I've said, and behave yourself."

As if I should feel like doing anything naughty on such a tragic evening!

It was only after she had left that I wondered how Nicholas, Sid, Picaroon and Luke were all to fit on the motor-bike.

The house was very silent and eerie now I was alone in it, but I found Gambler and Chiffon and they were very sympathetic.

Mrs. Tubb wasn't very long, and when she came back we had a game of bagatelle to take our minds off things. She was far too sensible to suggest I should go to bed before Nicholas returned; and I didn't tell her that I couldn't see how Sid could bring Picaroon and Luke home on his motor-bike.

We were in the nursery and I could not prevent my eyes straying to the two photographs we have of Auntie Gay, which stand on the chimney-piece. One shows her jumping Jubilee at Dublin Horse Show last summer; she is riding with the perfect forward seat and Jubilee is looking very dramatic with her dark tail streaming out behind. Auntie Gay is wearing a crash cap in this photograph and she looks very young and determined. She doesn't look quite so nice in the other one because she is wearing a bowler; but it is a very picturesque hunting photograph and Harvester is looking marvellous. I wondered if her face was very ashen now and if she would ever look the same again after such a serious illness.

Then we heard the back door open and Nicholas's voice called, "Hallo!"

"Have you got him?" I yelled, and he called, "Yes, come through and I'll tell you all about it."

This was an occasion for a pot of tea, and Mrs. Tubb was in her element. She fetched a fruit cake from the larder and then Nicholas reminded her we had had no tea or supper, so she fried us eggs and bread, and she and Sid had the cake and tea, and we had a sort of supper.

Nicholas told me he had found Luke crouching in the bracken soon after I had left, and he had started to walk home carrying the cat and leading Picaroon and The Black Demon. He had covered nearly three miles when Sid turned up, so the motor-bike was not much help, but it was nice to have company, and Sid had carried the miaowing Luke.

While we ate our supper Mrs Tubb very kindly fed the dogs and Luke, and agreed that Picaroon and Luke could spend the night together on twin rugs in the kitchen.

And so the first day of the holidays ended and, in spite of all my worries about Auntie Gay, I fell asleep a few minutes after I scrambled into bed and I slept long and well.

CHAPTER TWO

IT WAS after breakfast the next day. Mummy and Daddy had arrived home at half-past eight and made a valiant effort to appear cheerful, which did not deceive Nicholas or me at all. We soon discovered that Auntie Gay was still on the danger list and, presently, we started to discuss the fate of her animals.

"But it would be so easy, Mummy," said Nicholas. "We've two loose-boxes just waiting to be filled by two horses, and Clare and I have reached a sensible age now. We're quite competent and we have ridden Harvester and Jubilee several times. When you consider how much Auntie Gay has done for us you *must* see that the least we can do is to look after her animals while she is in hospital. I'll pay for their keep out of the money you put into savings for me during the war."

Mummy, tall, fair and elegant, said: "I don't think you realise how much you would be taking on. It would be a tremendous responsibility. If they were a couple of quiet ponies like Captain Pike's I would say yes, like a shot. But Harvester and Jubilee are worth over a thousand each and they are famous, and you've really had no experience. Auntie Gay would be heartbroken if anything happened to them; they are all she has. Don't you think it would be so much better if you just looked after Picaroon and Luke, and the horses went to a good livery stable?"

"Auntie Gay is broke. She couldn't afford to pay eight guineas a week for their keep," said Nicholas firmly, pushing his dark hair out of his eyes with a gesture of despair.

"Please let us have them. I *know* we can look after them. Please," I said.

"But what do you know about feeding and mucking out?" asked Mummy, and I knew then she was wavering.

"Lots," replied Nicholas convincingly. "We've watched Pauline. She's wizard at it."

Hypocrite! I thought. "We'll manage everything," I said. "Mr. Middleton will help us. He's got lots of straw and hay. Oh, do let us!"

"We will lead them over here. Auntie Gay often allowed us to lead them out on the roads to graze the verges, so she must have trusted us. Honestly, Mummy, we'll be dreadfully careful," promised Nicholas.

"The souls of caution," I added.

"All right, then. I give up. I've got to get back to Flaxborough, anyway so I've no more time for arguing. I wish your father could have put off his appointment in town to-day. He might have known a livery stable or something. You can have Harvester and Jubilee for a day or two and see how you get on. But you are not to do anything silly or rash. Do you hear, Nicholas? I've enough to worry about with Auntie Gray's peritonitis, without having to worry about her horses and you as well. I shall be back this evening, and you are both to do as Mrs. Tubb tells you." Mummy got to her feet with a long exasperated sigh. "I don't know why these things have to happen," she said.

"Then we can fetch the horses?" persisted Nicholas.

"Yes, I said so. Now don't be dumb. And don't go killing yourself or taking silly risks. Remember how much those two horses mean to Auntie Gay."

"Thank you! We certainly shall! Will you ring us

up at lunch time and let us know how Auntie Gay is?" I asked.

"I'll try," said Mummy.

A few moments later she had gone and we were silent, thinking of the hospital again.

"We've taken on a terrific responsibility," said Nicholas at last.

"Are you getting cold feet?" I asked.

"No, of course not. We jolly well ought to be able to look after a couple of horses."

"I hope they won't be as difficult as Luke," I said. For Nicholas had been kept awake all night by Luke's heart-rending miaows and this morning the cat would touch no food. Chiffon hated him, but one stare from his large, incredibly blue eyes would prevent her from coming to close quarters. We soon found Luke could out-stare anyone; he must have had a very clear conscience and, in the presence of other animals, he never lost dignity. Being a fairly well-trained Siamese cat, he would walk a little on a collar and lead, so I was able to take him for a stroll round the garden before Nicholas and I left again for Cherry Tree Cottage.

"If Stephen loses his chain this morning I'll murder him and you'll have to walk," threatened Nicholas, as we pedalled slowly down the leafy, winding road to Valleys End. Spring was here at last and the banks were decked with daffodils. The wet fields were very green and all the world smelled lovely after the night's rain. I forgot about poor Auntie Gay and felt quite wildly happy. I left go of the handle-bars and sang "Tipperary" out of tune; and Stephen took advantage of my mood and ran me into a bank.

Nicholas was *furious* and I suppose I couldn't really blame him.

"You just don't attend to what you are doing," he told me, as I scrambled to my feet. "You ruin all our

18

I could not bridle Jubilee

expeditions and how you are going to be able to look after Jubilee when you are so scatter-brained and hopeless I just don't know. I suppose Stephen's chain is off."

It *was*.

"Oh, don't be so cross," I said. "It's awful to be angry on such a lovely day. I've grazed my knees and cut my thumb. I'm frightfully sorry."

"You always are," said Nicholas grimly. "Is the chain off?"

"I'm afraid it is," I admitted. "I do *hate* bicycles. You've only got to take your mind off them for a minute—"

"Yes, I know, they run you into something," interrupted Nicholas. "Now I shall get filthy, oily and horrid. Harvester will hate it. This is positively the *last* time I put Stephen's chain back. Next time *you'll* have to do it and that will serve you right."

He fixed it and twenty minutes later we reached Cherry Tree Cottage and the horses greeted us with loud whinneys. We gave them each a feed and mucked out the stable, leaving the straw heaped in a corner. Then we fetched the tack from the saddle-room.

And now the trouble began. I could not bridle Jubilee; she put her head miles up out of my reach and Nicholas, who was having difficulty with Harvester, wouldn't come and help. I tried standing on a bucket and standing in the manger, but with no avail, and for an awful moment I wondered whether Mummy was right after all and we had not had enough experience. Then Nicholas suggested we should lead the horses in their head-collars and carry the bridles. It seemed rather feeble to give up so soon, but it was already after half-past eleven and we were afraid of being late for lunch, so we followed this suggestion and set out for home.

Jubilee was very fresh and very fit; and she danced and pranced and trod on my toes. I felt small and rather powerless and felt I would be safer riding than walking.

Nicholas managed Harvester beautifuly and he walked well ahead of me, swinging his arms and whistling an irritating tune. At intervals I yelled to him to wait, and he accused me of being a slow-coach, when I caught up, until I nearly lost my temper. However, in spite of all this, I thought Jubilee a wonderful exchange for the soulless Stephen. She was so superbly graceful with her long lovely neck, dark romantic mane and sparkling eyes, and every now and then she would kink her tail, sniff the air and snort like a wild mustang on the prairies.

"She needs more exercise," said Nicholas, knowingly. "She's younger than Harvester and not so wise.

Auntie Gay always said she was highly strung and difficult."

"Don't tell Mummy that whatever you do," I said.

It took us an hour and a half to walk the eight miles home and the time passed very quickly. Mr. Wise, who helps with the garden, had very kindly taken all the junk out of our loose-boxes, which made them look very bare. Jubilee was reluctant to enter hers; she stood on the threshold with her feet braced, snorting, and Nicholas had to help me. Once inside, she became very excited and dashed round and round, calling for Harvester, and we became so afraid she would jump out that we decided to shut the top door.

I was very worried that she might slip up and fall, because there was no straw on the floor, and we hurried round to the next-door farm to see Mr. Middleton.

"He's sure to be able to help us. He's always so terribly agreeable. But I do hope he will be quick. It will be so awful if Jubilee gets cast," I said.

"I can't see why she can't be sensible like Harvester," complained Nicholas, and I realised that in future he was going to consider me responsible for Jubilee's behaviour.

We found a farm labourer in the yard and he told us Mr. Middleton was out and would not be back till evening.

I said, "Oh, gosh, how awful." And Nicholas said, "I say, do you think he would lend or sell us a little straw, please? It's urgent."

The farm labourer stopped forking manure for a moment and said we had better wait till evening and see Mr. Midleton then. It happened they were very short of straw on the farm and were having to buy all their own. I could hear Jubilee neighing and clattering round the loose-box at home and I became frantic, so

21

I said, "But surely you could just lend us a little bit now. We can carry it back with us—just enough for one loose-box, please."

"Well, two loose-boxes actually," added Nicholas. "Only one is really urgent, though. We are afraid the horse is going to slip up. You see, her owner is ill. . . ." I told him then about Auntie Gay.

"It would be so awful if anything happened to her horses," I finished.

The farm labourer was silent for a minute or two and I thought he was going to relent, but in the end he only said, "The trouble is it isn't mine to lend."

"But surely Mr. Middleton wouldn't mind us having just a little bit," said Nicholas persuasively. "After all, he does know us."

"It's very short this year. We 'aven't 'ad enough for our own calves, otherwise I would let you 'ave some right away. But I can't really. Things being as they are and 'im down at the market."

"Isn't there *anything* you could lend us just to put on the floor," I asked. And I thought of Jubilee slipping on the Staffordshire bricks and breaking her knees.

"Would a bit of old musty 'ay do? Now I could let you 'ave some of that."

"Oh yes," I cried. "That's marvellous. Thank you so much. Where is it? Can we fetch it now, please?"

I wanted to say, "Quick. Hurry, before we are too late," and I could hear Jubilee neighing again.

The farm labourer was dreadfully slow. He straightened his back with a grunt, put down his fork and said, "You 'ad better follow me and we will see what we can do." Then he took us very slowly round two barns, through a cow byre and two gates into a second yard, where he showed us some dusty hay in a shed.

"You can take all you want of that and you're welcome to it," he told us.

I started to scoop it up in my arms.

"You'll spill masses like that," said Nicholas.

"Better take it in a couple of sacks," suggested the farm labourer.

"Oh yes, thanks. Where can we get them?" I asked.

"They're round the back of the barn. Come on; I'll show you," he said.

It took *ages* and all the time I was wondering whether Jubilee was hurting herself. But, at last, we had the sacks filled and were making for home and then we were opening her loose-box door and she was all right, though still in a desperate frame of mind. The hay wasn't enough to make a bed for her, but enough to stop her slipping on the bricks.

"Now what are we going to feed them on?" asked Nicholas, when we had finished spreading the hay.

"I suppose they need some more oats. A book I read said hunters needed fifteen pounds a day. I'm sure Pike's horses don't get that, though. If only these two hadn't been clipped in January we could have turned them out in the field," I said.

"I don't know; there's a cold wind. I think they could do on hay, actually, if we had any. We were fools not to bring some from Cherry Tree Cottage. We've been pretty scatter-brained," said Nicholas.

"I couldn't have carried hay as well as lead Jubilee," I told him. "Oh dear, we've left our bikes there, so we can't even bike over and get some."

"We shall have to hire a car," said Nicholas.

"But Mummy will be furious, and they are so expensive."

"We can't let the horses starve. It's our duty to Auntie Gay to feed her horses—whatever inconvenience it may put us to," said Nicholas in his definite tone of voice.

"Let's ask Mr. Wise if he has any suggestions." I ventured.

"He won't. He never does," retorted Nicholas.

"But, Nicholas, we can't possibly hire a car. Anyway, no taximan will want hay in his taxi," I said faintly.

"We'll hire a lorry, then."

"But that will be even more expensive."

"We'll hire a lorry and we'll have all Auntie Gay's hay, straw and oats transported here," cried Nicholas. "Why didn't we think of it before? We are absolute imbeciles! Of course, that's the answer."

"The expense," I muttered.

"I'll pay for it out of my savings if there is any argument. But there won't be. It's the obvious, sensible thing to do. Tubb, Tubb! Where are you? Do you know of anyone with a lorry, please? It's urgent . . . Tubb, Tubb!" He ran into the house calling Mrs. Tubb and I stayed in the sun calming Jubilee. I suppose elder brothers are useful sometimes, I thought. He's quite right. It's the obvious thing to do.

"It's all right," I told the grey head at my side. "We'll soon have plenty of hay and oats and straw here for you. Don't worry, we'll look after you."

And Jubilee looked at me with her great liquid eyes, and then nuzzled my pockets in search of sugar or carrots.

"That's done, I've telephoned," said Nicholas, coming back.

"Mr. Saunders—or young George Saunders, as Tubb calls him—is collecting the hay, straw and oats this afternoon."

"What time?" I asked.

"Oh, I don't know—just this afternoon."

"I hope it won't be five o'clock, because Jubilee's terribly hungry. We had better take them along the roadside."

"Not now," said Nicholas, "because Tubb says you're to come into lunch; it's past one o'clock."

We ate quickly, but were held up by Chiffon and Picaroon, who had a fight. It was Nicholas's fault because he gave Picaroon tit-bits from his plate and ignored Chiffon, who is a very jealous character. We had to throw water over the dogs to stop them and then we had to mop up the floor afterwards, so it was after two o'clock when we eventually returned to the stables.

It was simply wonderful to walk down the garden path and see two horses' heads looking over the loose-box doors and Jubilee greeted me with a tiny whinney. We had managed to persuade Mrs. Tubb to give us some oatmeal and a few rolled oats, so we fed them on these for a few moments; and then Nicholas said we might as well take them out on the roadside. Jubilee had suddenly become more obliging, and she put her head down when she saw me approaching with her head-collar.

"I think we are going to manage beautifully," I told Nicholas, as we led our two handsome horses down the drive. "If only Auntie Gay had just gone away for a holiday, instead of being ill, how wonderful everything would be."

"Don't speak too soon," warned Nicholas. And I wondered why my brother and I never feel enthusiastic at the same moment. We must have contrary natures, because when Nicholas is gay or reckless I am always gloomy and cautious, and vice versa. So we are forever damping each other's spirits.

The sun seemed to have abandoned the day and

there was a cold wind blowing now with a hint of snow in the air, which made me shiver.

"We must keep the horses moving or they'll catch a chill," said Nicholas. "Harvester doesn't seem very hungry."

"Jubilee is starving," I said.

We let them wander slowly, eating, up the road; and soon we had covered nearly a mile, and we heard the clatter of hoofs.

"Oh, gosh! Who's coming? Sounds quite a crowd. Don't say it's the riding school!" Nicholas exclaimed, halting Harvester.

"I hope not. We both look dreadfully dirty and untidy," I said, looking at Nicholas's ancient canvas trousers, procured in Brittany the summer before, his unsuitable sandals and dark tangled hair.

"You're not dressed for the part at all. You should have breeches and brogues."

"Well, what about you—a ski-ing jacket is far from correct wear and your slacks are far too bright for stable work," he replied.

"Oh, well, I don't care what she thinks."

They came into view, a string of riding school ponies with Pauline at the head.

"Derek's there and Dick," called Nicholas.

"Look, there's Magpie. Oh, I do *wish* she was mine," I said.

Presently they reached us, and Pauline looked down from Captain Pike's tall hunter, Guardsman, and said, "Well, well, well! ! You look as though you've got your hands full, Clare. What's happened to Gay Field? She must be in a very poor way to leave them to you to graze at the roadside. Steady, there, steady! Hasn't she any hay? It's too cold for clipped horses."

I couldn't answer, because Jubilee was dancing

around and trying to speak to the other horses, and it was all I could do to control her.

"Auntie Gay is ill," said Nicholas very stiffly. "So we are looking after them for her. She likes them to have a bite of spring grass at this time of year."

"Have you got them at your place then?" asked Pauline.

"But how wizard! Can you ride them?" called Derek.

"Yes, we have two loose-boxes—very nice roomy ones, too," replied Nicholas with dignity.

Pauline looked incredulous. "But—oh, well, I wish you luck. Take care, Clare. Turn her round," was all she said; and then with a clatter of hoofs the class had gone.

"I don't think she's so bad," I said to Nicholas.

"She was jolly condescending," he replied.

"She wasn't. You imagine things. She was only surprised," I told him.

"Nonsense. She was beastly. . . . That insinuation about Auntie Gay being in a poor way to leave them to us!"

"Well, it's true. She *is* in a poor way," I said.

"Do you think we had better take them back now? Jubilee is too excited to eat and it's getting colder."

We turned for home and when we reached the loose-boxes we found George Saunders unloading hay and putting it into Daddy's workshop. We gave cries of horror and I let go of Jubilee, who galloped away across the garden, breaking two cloches. I rushed after her and then I heard a dreadful sound—the car horn. Our parents were arriving back from Flaxborough! I felt dreadful and I was sure they wouldn't understand how everything had happened. They would think we had arranged for the hay to be put in the workshop.

I caught Jubilee quite easily and led her slowly and

dismally back to the stable. Nicholas was explaining, and George Saunders was taking the hay out of the workshop, with a pained expression on his face.

"I thought he understood. I said the back half of the garage on the telephone," Nicholas was telling the parents. "We had to do something about food for the horses."

The parents seemed to be taking it quite agreeably, so I approached Daddy and said, "I'm dreadfully sorry, but Jubilee has broken two of your cloches. It was my fault, not hers. I'll pay for new ones out of my savings."

"What's that?" he asked, swinging round. I repeated my confession and offer of payment, and he said he couldn't think why he had such awful children and I had better tell Wise about the cloches.

I said, "Sorry." And then he told us Auntie Gay was much better and off the danger list.

"We told her you had taken over the animals and, oddly enough, she seemed pleased. She said you were quite competent—an extraordinary woman," remarked Daddy.

CHAPTER THREE

WE WAKENED next morning to find a white world of snow, dazzling under heavy grey winter skies. April and spring seemed to have fled together overnight, driven by the strong bitter wind, and we were in the midst of winter once more.

"Wake up, Nicholas," I cried, running to my brother's bedroom. "The world's gone mad; there's deep snow everywhere." He turned slowly in bed and said, "Don't be funny, Clare. I'm sleepy. It's not April the first. Do leave me alone."

"It's eight o'clock," I told him sternly. "And if you don't believe me, just look out of the window and see for yourself."

I went away and fed Gambler and Picaroon— Mrs. Tubb had adopted Luke, who spent all his days on the kitchen chimney-piece, looking like a china ornament —and then I visited the horses. Poor Jubilee looked very dirty compared with the snow and I promised she should have a bath as soon as the weather was warmer. I gave them each a feed of oats and a bucket of water, and then I went in to breakfast. Nicholas was very excited by the snow and talked of tobogganing, but our parents said it would soon melt and, anyway, Harvester would take up all his time.

After breakfast more snow fell with the driving wind and we became very cold mucking out the stables, which took us nearly an hour.

"We can't take the horses out in this weather," said Nicholas. "It's much too cold."

We bedded them down in deep straw and gave them each a large pile of hay and then we groomed them. Jubilee was rather ticklish and I had to tie her up before I could brush her tummy, but she loved having her mane and head done.

Harvester disliked the dandy brush, but was otherwise excellently behaved, and soon his liver chestnut coat shone like a bronze medal.

We both got a tremendous thrill from having the horses to groom, and Nicholas wanted to invite Derek and Dick to tea to see how well they looked. I think he hoped they would pass the news on to Pauline.

We gave Harvester and Jubilee each another feed for lunch and made a rather amateurish wisp and wisped them, because Nicholas said it was our duty

29

to keep them really fit, so Auntie Gay could jump them as soon as she was out of hospital.

Jubilee hated being wisped and dashed round and round her loose-box with her ears laid back, so I fetched a head collar again to tie her up. But this time she was determined to be naughty and she put her head right out of my reach and eventually Nicholas had to come to my aid again, which was infuriating.

He said I was being feeble and should bang more with the wisp and keep my arm straight, and I said he was cruel and making Jubilee very angry. We argued for a while and then we went tobogganing on the big hill and met Dick and Derek, who started riding with Pauline at the same time as us.

"How are the two chargers?" called Dick.

"Fine, thank you," yelled Nicholas.

"Pauline thinks Gay Field must be a lunatic to let you look after them," said Dick, getting off his toboggan and coming up to us.

"Does she think we are terribly incompetent?" I asked.

"She says you know absolutely nothing about stable management and you couldn't possibly ride them," replied Dick.

"They are smashing horses!" said Derek.

"We've ridden them lots of times at Cherry Tree Cottage with Auntie Gay looking on," Nicholas said.

"Jubilee's a wonderful ride—so bouncy. She's super," I told them.

"Pauline and I have never got on, actually," remarked Nicholas.

"You're telling me," said Derek.

The snow was falling fast and lying on the side of the hill in a great drift. It was bad for tobogganing. One needed goggles to keep the snow out of one's eyes. Two grown-ups, walking slowly up the hill, told us it was dangerous, and we decided to go home. "It's time to give the horses their tea, anyway," I said.

We gave the stables a quick muck-out and then mixed Jubilee and Harvester each another feed. They didn't seem very hungry and had left most of their hay.

"It means they're getting enough; that's the main thing," said Nicholas.

Next morning a slow thaw had set in, and by afternoon we had decided to ride the horses. Jubilee was difficult to saddle, but Mr. Wise helped me. We took them out into the yard to mount and Mr. Wise gave me a leg up, nearly throwing me over the other side of the saddle with his strong arms.

We made a fine clatter as we trotted away down the drive. The horses were both very fresh and it was all we could do to stop them cantering. Jubilee was certainly very different from Magpie and each stride threw me out of the saddle. Nicholas was looking marvellous on Harvester, who was snatching at the bridle and dancing from side to side of the road.

We took a lane which led down into the little village of Appleby Green. There was a lot of snow here and the horses slipped a good deal, and then, half-way down the lane, we rode into a deep drift. The horses floundered, and thinking of bogs, I started to dismount, but Nicholas yelled, "Don't get off. You'll drown in it. It's about six feet deep! We had better turn back."

We started to retrace our footsteps and Jubilee became quite uncontrollable: she wanted to gallop, and when I held her back she ran backwards or leaped high in the air. Eventually, I slipped off and then Nicholas said I had better have Harvester and he would ride Jubilee. I said, no, I would have another

31

Nicholas was finding her rather difficult

try, but he insisted—so we swopped horses. I felt simply miles up on Harvester and I could see over all the hedge-tops; he had a very long stride and was much smoother than Jubilee.

Nicholas was finding her rather difficult; his stirrups seemed too long and he looked thoroughly uncomfortable; in fact. I thought I had managed her better myself.

"You look simply teeny up there," called Nicholas. "How do you like him? He's a much better ride than this silly grey animal, isn't he?"

"I like Jubilee best," I replied firmly.

We reached the road and then suddenly Harvester's quarters seemed to drop; his back seemed to contract and his hindlegs hardly worked at all. I panicked, certain he was going to collapse and die.

"Nicholas, Nicholas, stop! Look at Harvester," I yelled.

My brother is not quick in the uptake. "What's the matter now?" he shouted. in exasperated tones. "*Do* catch up."

"I can't," I yelled. "It's his hindlegs. Oh, *do* stop! It's awful."

I leaped to the ground and jarred my feet horribly on the hard road; and Harvester stood looking wretched and stiff, with his hindquarters drooping. I thought of Auntie Gay and how terrible it would be if her favourite horse died. Who would break the news to her? And I wished Pauline or Captain Pike would come along the road.

Nicholas turned Jubilee round and rode back. "What on earth is the matter?" he asked.

"Look," I said, "just look. Can't you see?"

He stared, and after a few moments he said, "You mean there's something wrong with his quarters?"

"I'll walk him on. . . . Watch."

I led the big liver chestnut horse a few steps, and Nicholas said, "It's cramp. Poor old fellow. We had better lead him home."

"You don't sound very perturbed," I remarked.

"Well, he's not dying. The main thing is to get him back to bed. You have Jubilee. I'll lead him," said Nicholas.

Jubilee wouldn't stand to be mounted and, when at last I was in the saddle, she cantered me home, much to Nicholas's disgust.

I felt rather miserable as I unsaddled and unbridled her. Nothing was turning out right and I was very worried about Harvester.

"We shall have to tell Mummy. I hope she won't think it is all our fault," I said to Nicholas.

"I don't see how she can. It's not as though we galloped him about the countryside. We were only

33

walking. She's not back from Flaxborough yet, though. The car's still out."

We wandered indoors and sat about the house looking disconsolate. "Supposing he dies," I said.

"Pessimist! Of course he won't. It's only a touch of cramp."

"It might be lockjaw. Supposing he's got a little puncture somewhere and we've never noticed it?"

The thought filled me with such horror that I leaped to my feet and started running to the stables.

Nicholas's voice followed me. "Why do girls always flap?" it asked.

I took off Harvester's rugs and searched him all over, but I could not find a scratch or puncture anywhere. I felt wonderfully relieved as I re-rugged him, but determined to have the vet. Otherwise, I knew I would worry all the night and the next day, even if the cramp disappeared completely.

I went indoors again and told Nicholas we must ring up the vet. He said we couldn't before we had seen Mummy, because vet's fees were expensive. I said I would pay them out of my savings and he said I was being ridiculous and flapping. We had a short argument, and then Nicholas, to my great surprise, gave in.

"All right. Go on, ring him up, then. Only don't ask me to explain everything to Mummy," he said.

Luckily we knew Auntie Gay's vet. His name is Hill; he is elderly, kind and has a soft voice which animals like.

He was not at his surgery when I telephoned, so I left a message asking him to call in at our place as soon as possible.

"Now we shall just have to wait. Oh, how awful!" I said to Nicholas.

We mucked out the stables again and bedded the

horses down in mostly new clean straw to impress Mr. Hill, and then we gave them another feed each and a little more hay. Jubilee was very excitable and *would* dig up the straw as soon as I spread it, which was *infuriating*. When I tried to change her rugs she bucked all round her stable like a bronco.

"She's mad, that horse," said Nicholas. "I would rather have old Harvester any day."

"She never does this sort of thing with Auntie Gay. It must be our fault. She used to be so sensible when I groomed her at Cherry Tree Cottage," I said.

And I remembered how quietly she had stood for Auntie Gay and how I had crawled under her grey legs, brushing her fetlocks.

"I don't see why we shouldn't have a tea-party quite soon, you know," said Nicholas. "We could have Derek, Dick, Wendy and Bobbie."

"Oh, not Bobbie. She's awful," I objected.

"I don't think she's bad. She's jolly sporting. Look how she manages that awful pony, Tinker. And she never complains how ever often she falls off," argued Nicholas.

I thought of Bobbie, her untidy brown hair, her mocking blue eyes and her legs and arms, which always seemed to be waving around like windmills. She was fearless and outspoken and rather pleased with herself.

Mr. Hill arrived in a large black car.

"So you are in charge of Miss Field's jumpers, are you? A big responsibility," he said. "And what's wrong to-day?"

"The liver chestnut, sir," replied Nicholas. "We led him out for a walk and he had attacks of cramp. As far as I know he never had that sort of thing when my aunt was looking after him."

"Bring him out, will you?" asked the vet.

Of course, Harvester seized this opportunity to be difficult, and he put his head out of Nicholas's reach, making us both feel very incompetent. We tried clumsily to grab his ears and then I offered him bread out my my pocket, but all to no avail. Presently, Mr. Hill came to our rescue, and then Harvester, listening to the vet's soft voice, put his head down and behaved beautifully.

"How many oats have you been giving these horses?" asked Mr. Hill.

"Three or four feeds a day, not more than fifteen pounds a day," I said.

"We want to keep them fit, because Auntie Gay will want to jump them as soon as she's out of hospital," added Nicholas. (There was no need to explain about our aunt's peritonitis; everyone in the horsy world seemed to know.)

"But you are not giving them much exercise, are you? . . . About an hour a day?"

"Less, I'm afraid," said Nicholas, leading Harvester out.

The horse was still stiff in the quarters.

"Exactly how much exercise has he had?" asked the vet.

"Nothing the day Auntie Gay went, eight miles walking the next day, nothing the following day and ten minutes to-day," said Nicholas.

"He's very hard," said Mr. Hill, "very hard and very fit."

"What's the matter? Is it serious?" I asked, for I felt I could not wait another moment for the verdict.

"It's a form of muscular cramp," explained the vet slowly. "You see, this horse has got very fit and has then been left to stand in the stable without any cut in his feed. It's nothing very serious—got any meadow hay?"

"Only mixture, I think," I said.

"Well, get some very soft meadow. Feed him on that—no oats—and give him a lot of slow walking. He'll be as right as rain in a day or two. You're a crazy couple of kids to give him fifteen pounds of oats a day. Not many horses, even if they are hunting hard, need as much. What's the grey been having? The same amount?"

"I'm afraid so," I owned, feeling very sheepish.

"You had better not tell your Auntie Gay. It would give her a heart attack. It's a wonder the mare hasn't blown up. Bring her out, will you? Let's have a look at her."

Of course, we had the usual trouble with the head-collar, and Nicholas nearly lost his temper with me, but at last we had it on and I led her out of the box. She was very excited to be in the drive again and started to paw up the gravel.

"Don't you give that mare another grain of oats," said the vet firmly. "She's fat and will keep fit enough on the hay you've got. There are some horses which do well on very little corn and she's one of them. How about exercise—can you manage to ride her?"

"Yes," said Nicholas quickly. "We used to help Auntie Gay exercise her sometimes. Clare has ridden her quite a lot, haven't you, Clare?"

I wanted to ask Mr. Hill's advice on how to control her when she started to run backwards, but Nicholas gave me a look which meant "say yes."

So I said, "Yes, often."

"Well, don't give her less than an hour and a half a day," said the vet firmly. "I'll be round to look at Harvester again to-morrow."

When he had left, I said, "Oh, dear! We are *hopeless*, but I should have thought a big horse like that would have been all right with that amount of oats."

37

"One can only learn by bitter experience," said Nicholas.

"I'm going to buy another book on stable management. Our one definitely says a hunter can have fifteen pounds a day," I complained.

"Yes, but don't you see? It means a hunter which is hunting," explained Nicholas. "You must learn to put a head-collar on Jubilee, by the way."

I nearly pointed out *he* had not been able to put one on Harvester at the crucial moment and then I thought any comment would only lead to an argument.

When our parents returned we had to confess about Harvester's cramp, and Mummy got into rather a flap and insisted on ringing up Mr. Hill and discussing it with him.

"I knew this sort of thing would happen. I do wish we had sent the horses to a reliable stable," she said.

In the evening Chiffon and Picaroon had another fight, which exasperated our parents. Picaroon tore Chiffon's ear and Chiffon bruised and cut Picaroon's eyelid. We spent a long time bathing their wounds and dressing them with some penicillin powder, which the vet had given us for Gambler when he cut his leg some weeks before.

By bed-time I was feeling rather fed up with the animals. But I wrote a long letter to Auntie Gay, telling her about Harvester's cramp, but not mentioning any of our other difficulties, because I did not want to worry her.

I wondered whether Nicholas and I would manage to exercise Jubilee successfully on the morrow, and when I slept I dreamed she bucked me off into a bramble bush, galloped away across a field and then turned into an elephant.

CHAPTER FOUR

"Y OU'VE GOT to exercise Jubilee to-day," said Nicholas next morning, in matter-of-fact tones. "I don't know what she will be like without Harvester. Where on earth shall I go for an hour and a half," I wondered.

"I'll gladly swop with you," suggested Nicholas. "I don't fancy a lot of slow walking."

"I don't want to swop," I said. "But couldn't we sort of help each other? I mean, we could take a bike as well."

"I don't think I need any help leading Harvester about the countryside, thanks. And I don't fancy biking around after you on Jubilee. Besides, our bikes aren't here."

Wishing I had a more helpful brother, I said, "Oh, well, never mind; I'll be all right."

"What are you worrying about?" asked Nicholas. "You've ridden Jubilee lots before. You never used to be nervous. If you are scared, *I'll* ride her. I thought you were dying to take her out."

I thought I detected scorn in his voice.

"Of course I'm not scared," I said hotly. "I only thought you might like to ride her half-way. I mean, not being able to ride Harvester."

"Well, I shan't have time, actually, because I'm going round to see Derek and Dick. But, for goodness' sake, ride properly if you meet Pauline. Don't make a fool of yourself again. You let us down horribly the other day."

"You are horrid," I said, and I thought: why must boys always want to impress people?

"All the children from the riding school will be crowing now," he added.

"You are too jolly sensitive! Anyway, none of them could have stopped Jubilee from dancing around. Besides, I don't claim to be an expert. I haven't a reputation to keep up," I told him.

"Nor have I," said Nicholas. "Only I see this as a sort of challenge. Pauline and all her pupils think we are totally incapable of looking after Auntie Gay's horses. They think Auntie Gay is a lunatic to let us have them. I want to prove she is not."

"It's a good thing they didn't hear about the oats. I hope they don't have the same vet," I said, and then I went outside to muck out, groom and saddle and bridle Jubilee.

She seemed quieter this morning and very disappointed when she found she was not to have a breakfast of oats. Nevertheless, I was a little apprehensive. I had only ridden her occasionally and always with Auntie Gay. I had no idea how she would behave when hacking alone after so little work. It would be a strange piece of country for her, too, and she had always been inclined to shy. . . . Boys have so little imagination, I thought, remembering how unhelpful Nicholas had been—they don't realise what a difference change of environment can make to a horse.

Jubilee would not stand still to be mounted and eventually I had to enlist Nicholas's assistance, which I had not meant to do. He seemed a little perturbed now by Jubilee's obvious excitement.

"I say, do you think you're going to be all right? I will come out too, if you like," he said.

But I had made up my mind I would do without him.

"Thanks. I can manage quite well," I replied coldly. And I trotted down the drive and out into the road, before remembering that one should always walk a horse for at least half a mile after leaving the stable.

It was one of those freak spring days; as hot as summer and smelling like heaven; and yet the sun's warm gold fell on bare boughs and wintry hedgerows; and the naked branches of the tall elms looked bizarre against the deep blue of the skies. It was a day of gold, of brown and blues and greys, strangely lacking in the myriad greens one associates with the English spring. But in spite of the heat there was a lightness in the air which kept Jubilee on her toes. She was overjoyed to be out; she danced and she sidled, and she peeped at every little object at the roadside. I felt like a queen on a prancing Arab steed and I thought: this is a day I shall always remember; it will remain over the years crystal clear in the dark caverns of my mind. I shall bore my grandchildren with a description of it. On waking to find a grey winter day, I shall recall it and the skies will seem blue like these and the land golden with sunshine. I looked at Jubilee's delicate ears, her graceful head, and I thought: I am one of the luckiest children in the whole wide world. What other person of my age can ride like this on a horse which combines beauty with intelligence and good manners? And I quoted aloud:

> "The fleetness of the deer,
> The patience of the ox,
> The soft eye of the gazelle
> And the mane of the lion."

It was lovely to be so high up, to be able to see over garden walls and high fences, and to feel the energy and power of Jubilee between my legs and underneath me. I felt more part of her than I had ever felt part of Captain Pike's ponies. I felt I was riding better

41

than I had ever ridden before. I chanted from Whyte-Melville's poem:

"With a hopeful heart and a conscience clear,
I can laugh in your face, Black Care;
Though you're hovering near, there's no room for
*   you here,*
On the back of my good grey mare."

And Jubilee cocked back an ear and listened to me.

Then my thoughts turned to Auntie Gay and I wondered whether it was wrong to feel so happy, when my happiness was partly caused by her illness. But I felt sure she would want me to enjoy riding Jubilee.

We left the road and took a grassy track which led us up over the sunny southern shoulder of a hill and then dropped down into a hidden valley, which Nicholas and I call Hangman's Hollow and the map calls Fern Valley. Here the grass was greener and a few buttercups and daisies had broken into flower and, shaded by the hill, it was cooler.

There was an air of secrecy about this valley—something spooky, which made one hesitate to dally there too long. Jubilee was aware of it; she began to snort through her nostrils and canter sideways. I shortened my reins and she snatched at the bit, and my legs slipped back. Suddenly I was out of time with her. I lost the lovely feeling of cadence and control. She threw up her head and banged my nose and made my eyes water.

"Whoa, steady, Jubilee! Walk, walk," I said, shortening my reins again. The track now led us into a wood carpeted with bracken and last autumn's leaves. It was very quiet here and very still, and Jubilee slowed down to a trot. I patted her neck and began to wonder how Nicholas was managing Harvester.

Then suddenly she stopped dead in her tracks, uttering the most awful snort, and I could feel her trembling underneath me, and her heart beating. She sniffed the air and kinked her tail and stared with wide, startled eyes down the wood. It was a moment before I had collected my wits enough to speak to her. I spoke in calming tones and I thought she must have seen a ghost. Perhaps Nicholas and I were right and there is something mysterious and dreadful about this hollow. Jubilee cocked back an ear and listened to me for a moment, and then she swung round on her hocks and galloped back in the opposite direction. I nearly fell off; I don't know why I did not. I lost both stirrups and slipped to one side, and the bracken seemed very close to my head, but I managed to right myself and, as we reached Hangman's Hollow, I brought Jubilee to a standstill. She seemed to be in a hysterical frame of mind; she was trembling and had broken into a sweat; and, every now and then, she gave a little snort. I could not imagine what had upset her. I patted her neck and talked to her for a little while and then I started to walk her back into the wood. She was tense and her heart was thumping like mad. I could feel she was ready to swing round again at any moment.

I stared into the brown depths of the wood in the hope of seeing the ghost myself, until my eyes began to water again. But Jubilee was not exactly looking *into* the wood; she was peering round every corner, as though she expected something to jump out at her, and she was sniffing the air. I felt sure ghosts had no smell and I really could not understand her at all. She felt rather as though she was walking on springs and I knew she must be looking very lovely. Then she stopped again with a terrific snort and, following her line of vision, I saw a great white sow.

Then, in a moment, I remembered Auntie Gay telling me Jubilee was terrified of pigs. What a fool I had been to forget it! And I could smell the piggy smell myself now and hear the grunting of pigs farther ahead. I tried to collect my wits quickly, but I wasn't quick enough, and for the second time that day Jubilee galloped back down the wood.

I managed to stop her before we reached Hangman's Hollow and then I sat still and thought for a few minutes. Should I turn back and avoid an argument or try to go on and risk falling off and perhaps a big defeat? I tried to recall Auntie Gay's stories in detail, but I could not remember the end of any of them—though I felt sure she must have always succeeded in getting Jubilee past the pigs in some way or other. I felt very inexperienced and incompetent, and my mount was becoming impatient. She started to paw the ground, first with one hoof then with the other. And she was so obviously dying to go back through Hangman's Hollow that, in a sudden fit of contrariness, I decided we would face the pigs again.

"I'm going to show you they are all right. Come on, now, don't be an idiot. Walk on," I said, turning her round and taking the path into the wood once more.

"And this time," I added, "no turning back. Be brave, Jubilee, brave and courageous. It's only a great fat pig, too heavy to run."

But my words were of little avail. Her two rapid retreats seemed to have made her the more frightened. She didn't want to enter the wood, and it was a struggle to make her walk along the path at all. In fact, each step was preceded by a terrific snort of fear and I knew she was all ready for another flight. I sighted the great sow again, however, before Jubilee stopped dead in her tracks and so I felt I had advanced a little on my last attempt. I wished either Pauline or Captain Pike was here to advise me—or even Nicholas would have been a help. I felt so utterly alone and helpless. What should one do on these occasions? Jubilee seemed genuinely frightened, so sternness would be of little avail. On the other hand, my calming words and soothing pats seemed to have no effect at all. At last I decided to dismount and try leading her by.

"Look, Jubilee. I'm not afraid," I told her, slipping quietly from the saddle. I placed myself on her off-side, so I was in between her and the pig, and stood patting her neck for a few moments.

"I'll protect you from that silly old sow," I said, and my words seemed to give her confidence, because she gave me a little push and trembled less. I thought how wonderful she looked with her lovely arched neck, her dilated nostrils and dark startled eyes—like a picture I had seen in a gallery some months before, but better because she was real, alive and so full of the vitality which no picture can quite capture. Presently I tried to coax her forward and I was secretly congratulating myself on my success when, for the first time, the pig saw me. She fixed her little pink eyes on me for a moment and her mouth seemed to smile like a human's mouth; then suddenly she gave a squeal of delight and rushed towards Jubilee and myself. Then in a second all was lost. With one leap Jubilee had snatched the reins from my hands and was galloping back down the wood as fast as her legs would take her. I was left, mountless, staring at the cause of all the trouble, who obviously thought I was about to hand over her daily meal. I have never liked pigs very much, but since that day I have borne them a lasting grudge.

"Idiot, tactless idiot! I've no food for you!" I shouted to the sow and then I started to trudge back after Jubilee. She'll get killed now on the road, I thought, or at least break her bridle—then what shall I say to

Nicholas, Mummy and Auntie Gay? Grown-ups always say childhood is the happiest time of one's life, I reflected, but it seems to me everything goes wrong when you're a child and you've always got to be thinking of excuses to satisfy parents and relatives.

She won't be killed; dreadful things like that only happen to other people, not to you, Clare Field, I told myself. But she might slip and break her knees or strain her fetlock in a rabbit hole or roll on Auntie Gay's expensive saddle or just arrive home in time to frighten Nicholas and Mummy out of their wits. What *would* they say if she arrived outside the stable without me? Mummy would be so anxious she would be furious afterwards, even when she found I was all right.

No, that mustn't happen, I decided, beginning to run. I shall have to explain everything and not add any excuses—excuses never help anyone; they're a snare and delusion. But I mustn't let Mummy send Jubilee away.

I reached Hangman's Hollow and there was no sign of her, but I did not expect her to dally there. I found the road and looked up and down with a thumping heart. I called to a man on a bicycle but he had not seen her; and then I began to feel really anxious. If she had been a sensible sure-footed pony I would not have worried so much, but Jubilee, when alarmed and excited, would stop at nothing. She wouldn't think before she crossed a road, or proceed slowly where the tarmac was slippery.

I began to imagine what Nicholas would say when I returned without her. . . . "Oh, Clare how *could* you? But why did you dismount?" Or "Christmas! And where is she now? We've let Auntie Gay down! Mummy will never let us keep them after this; and Harvester will have to go as well." Or Nicholas might be kind, which would be worse; he might say, "Oh, never mind, Clare; these things happen to everyone. One only learns by bitter experience. I'm sure I couldn't have got her by the pigs. Mummy won't let us keep them now, even if we *do* find Jubilee, but these last few days have been wizard anyway." But I would know he was only hiding his disappointment and the dreadful feeling of having let Auntie Gay down.

She was standing by a five-barred gate, talking to a cart-horse

Two little boys came along the road and called out, "Lost your 'orse? Where's your 'orse, cowboy?"

I asked them if they had seen Jubilee and they said no, but they had heard hoofbeats a little way back.

I walked on towards home and then suddenly I saw her. She was standing by a five-barred gate, talking to a cart-horse; she looked very Arabian and very

47

self-possessed, and I felt annoyed with her for having caused me so much unnecessary worry.

I called her name and she turned her head to look at me with her beautiful calm eyes and then I couldn't feel cross any longer. I began to run, which is a silly thing to do because it often frightens horses, but she continued her conversation with the handsome cart-horse, who looked like a Clydesdale. One rein was broken but the rest of the tack was intact, and Jubilee hadn't a scratch.

I mounted quickly and set off for home, singing "Roll Out the Barrel" and "Hanging Out the Washing on the Siegfried Line," which Tubb had taught me when she was in a good mood.

I rounded a corner and met Pauline, who was biking to a field to fetch two ponies. She was wearing a scarf over her head—the mauve one, which Nicholas hates, and she had on drill trousers and black lace-up boots.

I don't think I am a very lucky person, but I do have strokes of good luck sometimes and I think this was one of them. If Pauline had come along seven or eight minutes earlier I would have wished the earth to swallow me up and I should never have looked Nicholas in the face again. But, as it happened, I was able to call out, "Good morning," as though I was returning from the most orderly ride in the world. And Pauline stopped her bike and said, "How are you getting along? She looks quiet enough now."

I didn't like to tell her the truth about the pigs, because of Nicholas, so I said, "Quite well, really. I find her a bit difficult occasionally, though. She doesn't like pigs much, but she's a lovely ride."

"A bit too much for you and Nick, I should think," said Pauline firmly. And I laughed secretly to myself, because Nicholas hates anyone besides Tubb to shorten his name, but Pauline is not nearly imaginative enough to think of things like that.

"We are learning a lot," I said. She gave me a look which meant, you need to, and then she remounted her bike and pedalled away.

I was late for lunch and Nicholas was waiting anxiously in the drive for me when I got back.

"At last!" he cried. "Do hurry. What has happened? Tubb's worried to death. If our parents had been at home there would have been a search party."

"Hypothesis! If my father was a horse he would win the Derby," I said, dismounting. "I couldn't help it. I'm sorry. I'll tell you about it at lunch."

"My dear Clare," said Nicholas with dignity, "Tubb and I have eaten. The time is precisely ten minutes past two. We don't flap for nothing."

"I had trouble with a pig and I met Pauline," I remarked as I put Jubilee in her box. I waited for Nicholas's exclamation of horror. It soon came.

"You mean, Pauline saw you? You didn't fall off in front of her? Oh, Clare, you didn't really? If you did it's the end. Everyone will know. Mummy will hear and the horses will have to go." He sounded so horrorstruck, I had to enlighten him at once.

I told him the whole story and he heaved a sigh of relief at the end.

"I suppose you wouldn't mind if I broke my neck, so long as Pauline didn't know," I said.

"Don't be silly," retorted Nicholas. "Of course I would care like anything. I've told you what I feel about Pauline. You've got no pride at all. You don't mind what people think, but I do and I'm not going to let down Auntie Gay."

We hurried indoors and I discovered I was ravenously hungry. Tubb had kept all the best bits of lunch for me; one really scores in our house by being late.

49

"In future I think we had better ride together," said Nicholas, as though he had just had a brilliant new idea. "Then we can give each other a hand in difficulties."

CHAPTER FIVE

"HARVESTER BEHAVED beautifully as usual," Nicholas told me as I scraped up the last of the apple pie, "and Derek and Dick are coming to tea the day after to-morrow."

"Oh, *no!*" I protested.

"What *is* the matter? They're perfectly harmless and dying to see our two charges. By the way, will you ask Bobbie and Wendy?"

"Can't we leave the tea-party until we are a little better at managing the horses?" I suggested. "I mean, we could have much more fun then."

"What *is* up with you, Clare? Honestly, you *have* become anti-social. Derek and Dick were most enthusiastic."

"I don't know. I just don't feel like a tea-party. They'll want to see how well I can manage Jubilee and I'm hopeless. Anyway, why don't *you* ask Bobbie and Wendy?"

"Because they're girls," said Nicholas promptly, "and it is more sensible for you to ask the girls. You don't want a party of boys, do you?"

"I don't want a party of anything," I declared defiantly. "Have you asked Mummy about it?"

"No, but she won't mind. She likes us to have lots of friends. Don't be such a spoil sport. *Do* ask them, Clare, please."

"I can't think why you suddenly want a party at all. You've never wanted Derek and Dick before," I said, but I knew I was beginning to weaken and Nicholas knew, too.

"You'll give them a ring then, will you?" he said. "That's wonderful. We'll have éclairs and meringues and a jam sponge filled with lashings of cream—one of Tubb's best."

"But I haven't said I will yet," I told him. "I don't like Bobbie at all."

But Nicholas continued, unperturbed, "And cucumber sandwiches and choclate fingers; and I'll play them my new record from *The Mikado*. It's going to be wizard, so long as you don't muff things or fall off."

"I'm not going to ride. I don't think it need be a riding sort of party. Let's listen to your records instead. We can exercise the horses in the morning," I suggested.

"But it's going to be a riding party. I've arranged that. Dick and Derek want to see Harvester over the sticks, as they put it."

"Nicholas! You're not going to jump Harvester?" I cried in horror. "You *can't*. Mummy will be furious. You would be letting down Auntie Gay. Supposing you jagged his mouth and spoiled him for all the shows this summer? You would be letting down England too, then."

"Don't get in such a flap! Only over a tiny jump, two feet high, silly. If I can't pop a horse over an obstacle of that height without spoiling him I deserve to be hanged, drawn and quartered," said Nicholas in calming accents.

I felt exasperated. "You don't just want to show off, do you?" I asked; and I regretted the spitefulness of the question immediately.

51

"No," said Nicholas. And then he walked out muttering that he must clean his tack.

I rang up Bobbie and Wendy and, to my sorrow, they both could come. Normally, I like having people to tea—especially people like Rosamund, who is a school friend of mine—but I dreaded this party, because I knew Wendy and Bobbie would want to see how well I could manage Jubilee and I had an inferiority complex about my riding.

I hoped Mummy would suggest postponing or putting off the party, but when we told her about it during the evening she was thrilled with the idea.

"But, Clare, it's a lot of work for Mrs. Tubb and it's only right you should help a bit with the sandwiches," she told me.

"I'll peel the cucumber and whip the cream," said Nicholas.

"Fortunately I can be at home that afternoon, so we should manage all right. By the way, if all goes well you can visit Auntie Gay in a few days' time. She's doing most awfully well now. The doctors are delighted. And she's dying to know how you are getting on with the horses," said Mummy.

That night in bed I made a resolution to school Jubilee in our paddock on the following day and to practise my riding. I was determined to give Auntie Gay a good report on our progress and to manage Harvester.

I started early, but I wasn't very successful and Jubilee seemed quite unreasonably excited. I tried with a loose rein, but she would not relax. Presently Nicholas joined me on Harvester, who was calm and sedate, and gave me advice in his elder-brother voice.

"I'm going for a hack now. I don't seem much good in the field," I said at last.

"I'll come too, just in case you meet pigs," said Nicholas. "The vet said yesterday that I could do at least an hour's slow riding. In fact, he was very pleased with Harvester."

"We *must* do something about getting some more meadow hay," I remembered suddenly. "That little bit you borrowed from Middleton won't last long."

"Gosh! I had forgotten all about that. I'll ring up Watts, the hay merchants, when I get home," said Nicholas.

We rode slowly in the clear spring sunshine and our grotesque shadows walked beside us. The horses seemed sleepy and contented, and Harvester's ears flopped to and fro with each stride.

The countryside was growing greener and more beautiful each day. The beeches and oaks were breaking into leaf at last and the cottage gardens were gay with spring flowers.

We were silent, alone with our own dreams and deep in thought, and the road was quiet and deserted. The clip-clop of the horses' hoofs, the voices of the birds and the gentle rustle of leaves and grasses in the wind were music in my ears. I wanted to ride on and on for ever in the sunlight along the twisty country road with Jubilee's long neck and little grey and black ears always before me.

Soon we turned off in the woods and, where the track was soft and suitable, we had a quiet canter—or rather Jubilee and I cantered and Nicholas walked on Harvester.

Then we took a track across a little undulating meadow and rode through a farmyard, where we met one of Daddy's acquaintances, a neat, trim, elderly man with white hair and a white moustache, called Major Tidy. We always laugh whenever we see him because of his name, and this occasion was no excep-

53

tion. We were both speechless with laughter, although we had been told many times by our parents that it was babyish and idiotic to laugh at him, because he had the misfortune to be called Tidy. But to make matters worse he always talks like a stock character in one of our books, and to-day he started right away by saying, "Well, I'll be jiggered, if it's not Nicholas and Clare on a couple of fine chargers!"

I did not look at Nicholas, but I knew he was turning red in the face with the effort of trying to suppress his laughter.

"Yes," I said, "yes, aren't they nice?" and then I gave a silly giggle and could say no more.

"I can see you two young rascals are laughing as usual," continued Major Tidy. "Do you look after these two fine chargers yourselves? . . . Elbow grease, a good old wisp and all that?"

"That's right, sir," said Nicholas, finding his voice at last. "They are the two show jumpers, you know them, I expect, Harvester and Jubilee. Gay Field is our aunt and she's ill, so we are looking after them."

"Of course, I know them, of course. But now let's look and see if the grooming is satisfactory," said Major Tidy, turning up Harvester's mane. Underneath he found the tell-tale dust and grease and suddenly I realised we were not very competent grooms; and, looking at Jubilee, I noticed her ears were coated with a thin layer of dirt which was shown up more clearly by the sunshine.

"You don't pass, you know. This is the great test, and look . . ." Major Tidy held up his hand, now grey with grease. "See. You can still learn something from an old man! I used to catch out my men this way time and time again in the old days. I got a reputation as a stickler, but my horses were the best turned-out in the Regiment."

54

Nicholas said, "Yes, sir. We are only beginners in this game." And then we said good-bye and rode on in silence.

A little breeze had sprung up from nowhere, and the air seemed cooler, and the leaves whispered to one another, and the grasses shivered.

"I suppose we haven't put much work into our grooming the last day or two," said Nicholas, looking at Harvester's large dusty ears.

"I think we've worked fairly hard on their necks and shoulders and forgotten the little awkward bits like under the mane and behind the ears," I said.

"Poor old Harvester!" laughed Nicholas. "First of all, we give you so much food and so little exercise that you get cramp and then we don't groom you properly and forget to wash behind your ears!"

"I expect they both wonder what on earth has happened to Auntie Gay and wonder whether they are to be left in our hands for the rest of their lives. Trust Tidy to find something wrong!" I said.

"It's really a jolly good thing," remarked Nicholas. "I would rather he noticed it than Pauline."

When we had returned home and unsaddled and unbridled the horses we started to groom them with dandy brushes. Jubilee was difficult and ticklish and I had to tie her up. She pawed the ground and gnashed her teeth whenever I brushed her tummy or flank, but was quieter when I used the body brush. I picked out her hoofs, because I had forgotten to do it earlier in the day and, by mistake, I poked her frog and then she lashed out and broke the glass of my watch and left a little bruise on my wrist.

Nicholas seemed more successful and devoted a long time to wisping Harvester, which he said, was the best way to muscle up horses.

After lunch we groomed the horses again and I vainly tried to brush Jubilee's ears.

"Do you think Auntie Gay really manages to get them clean?" I asked at last, in exasperation.

"Of course. You just haven't the knack. Let me do them. You don't think Auntie Gay would ride Jubilee at the White City with dirty ears, do you?" said Nicholas.

"Do you mean Auntie Gay's or Jubilee's ears?" I asked.

"Oh, come on. This is not the time for joking. Let me have a shot. Move over," said Nicholas, taking the dandy brush.

But he failed, too. And in the end we just wiped her ears with a damp rubber. "That will only take off the surface dust, but I think she'll turn crackers if we try any more," said Nicholas, looking at Jubilee as she dug up her bed of straw first with one hoof and then with the other.

"She's so highly strung," I said.

"Not highly strung, just plain spoilt. Look at her now—digging like mad; it's just temper," contradicted Nicholas.

"I'm sure Auntie Gay has never spoilt a horse in her life. It must be our mistake. We're doing something wrong," I said hotly.

We were near quarrelling, exasperated by our struggles with Jubilee, who had banged Nicholas's nose twice with her head and trodden on my left big toe three times.

"Perhaps we will be allowed to visit Auntie Gay soon and then she'll tell us what to do," I suggested.

"Don't be silly. We mustn't worry her. Once she starts worrying about her horses she'll never get well," argued Nicholas.

"I suppose it's better that Jubilee should go around

with dirty ears than Auntie Gay be fussed. It's really our pride which makes us take it all so seriously," I said.

Then we heard Mummy calling, "Tea."

CHAPTER SIX

WE GROOMED our horses for over an hour the next morning, and Jubilee was so ticklish that eventually I abandoned the dandy brush and only used the body brush. Afterwards we cleaned the tack.

By the time our guests arrived we had decided not to jump. It had rained a little in the night and the grass was still wet, so we said the ground in the field was too slippy and that made a good excuse. Bobbie brought Tinkerbell. Wendy brought Dawn, and Dick and Derek brought their new-fangled and nameless bicycles.

It was rather awkward because Bobbie and Wendy soon offered the twins a ride on Tinkerbell and Dawn, and yet I did not think I ought to offer them Jubilee. We rode down our own quiet road for nearly a mile and then we took a path at the side of a wheat field. The day was wild and gusty with gay little clouds vying with one another in an ever-changing sky. The old trees creaked and groaned, and the grasses and flowers held a silvery concert of their own.

Our sixteen hoofs squelched heavily in the muddy path and the bikes could only proceed slowly.

"What's Harvester like to ride? Pretty quiet and easy, I should think," asked Dick, kicking Tinkerbell until he was beside Nicholas.

"Oh, absolutely bang on! Streets better than anything I have ever ridden before. Clare and I are dashed lucky," my brother replied, and I thought how annoyed my parents would be if they had heard him say "Bang on."

"Lucky, yes. You're telling me!" exclaimed Dick with unconcealed envy. "And what about Jubilee? You find her a handful, don't you, Clare?"

"I did at first, but we understand each other better now," I told him.

"Can I try her?" asked Derek suddenly. And I didn't answer at once because I was in a whirl of indecision. It seemed awful not to say "yes." Our guests would think I was horribly selfish; yet if I explained that I was afraid they would not manage Jubilee they would immediately think me conceited. But, on the other hand, Auntie Gay had given me a lesson or two and knew I was riding her horse every day.

If Dick or Derek mounted Jubilee and gave her a couple of kicks which they used as aids when riding Captain Pike's ponies, she would shoot into a gallop and probably fall on the road and break her knees. Then I should never forgive myself; my parents would say I had been idiotic and Auntie Gay would be very annoyed to think I had been allowing my friends to ride Jubilee.

At last I said, "Well, you see . . ."

And then Nicholas came to my rescue. "Auntie Gay has only given *us* permission to ride her horses," he said. "I'm awfully sorry. But we haven't been allowed to see her since she was dashed off to hospital, so we couldn't possibly ask. And as they *are* so famous and valuable we daren't do anything without her permission."

"But if Clare can manage Jubilee, I'm sure *I* can. After all, Pauline did say my leg position was much better than hers," argued Derek.

58

"That's just the difference," said Nicholas—and I thanked goodness my brother was sharper-witted than myself. "Pauline's style of riding is quite different from Auntie Gay's. We try to practise Auntie Gay's style and so the horses *do* understand us a little, but if you ride them in Pauline's style, heaven help us!"

Just they we turned off the path and opened a gate into a large flat meadow.

"The ideal place for a gallop!" shrieked Bobbie. "You can keep Tinkerbell, Dick," she added generously, " 'cos I can gallop him every day."

"What about a race?" suggested Derek. "I'll be the starter. Bobbie, you can cycle across and judge the finish. Buck up, girl! Dawn and Tinkerbell must have a start, because they are so much smaller."

"You seem to be taking over the proceedings," remarked Nicholas, but his words, if heard, were ignored.

"You can have Dawn if you like," Wendy told Derek.

"It's all right, thanks. I want to be starter," he told her.

Feeling a spoilsport and prig, I said regretfully, "Jubilee is not supposed to race; it hots her up and she's so excitable."

"Oh, Clare! Don't ruin everything. We can't race with only three," cried Bobbie as she pedalled away across the field. And this time Nicholas did not come to the rescue.

"It won't hurt her just for once," he said. "I'm sure Auntie Gay would understand if she knew the circumstances." And then he gave me a meaning look, which meant: "This is a challenge"; and said in an undertone, "Only for pity's sake stop at the far gate, Clare!"

"All right." I agreed, grimly, not feeling equal to the situation at all.

"Line up," called Derek. "Are you ready? Get set! Go!"

We raced across the field faster than I had ever been in my life before, and I gave Jubilee her head and hoped for the best. Captain Pike's ponies had never been very willing to canter for me, let alone gallop, and my experience of fast riding was very small. The wind was in my face; it whistled past my ears and mingled with the thud of hoofs. Jubilee's long grey neck stretched before me; her ears lay flat and her dark mane was lifted by the wind.

I crouched forward and realised my stirrups were too long for galloping. We overtook Tinkerbell and then Dawn; and there was a long stretch of green before us. And soon we were neck and neck with Harvester.

"Come on, old fellow!" cried Nicholas.

"Faster, Jubilee!" said I.

The thrill of the race had hold of us now. Our prudence, our sense of judgement had been carried away with the wild west wind.

I urged Jubilee and she responded with a burst of speed, which was wonderful to feel. We gained a little and then Nicholas drove Harvester faster and we were neck and neck again.

My heart was thumping and I thought I could feel Jubilee's too, down by the girth, beating like mad with the joy and exertion of the race. I had forgotten Auntie Gay, forgotten my mount's excitable temperament and my own responsibilities.

I glanced at Nicholas. His face looked set and determined and he was riding with the correct forward seat —not crouching like myself. I urged Jubilee again and we gained once more in another glorious burst of speed. Never had I been so fast before; never had the wind raced past me like this! And then I saw Bobbie, a small figure with dark ruffled hair. I gave a final push with my legs and galloped past her, and then I saw ahead a new and treacherous barbed-wire fence glistening in the pale sunshine.

For one terrible moment, which I shall never forget, I thought Jubilee and I were about to impale ourselves on those bright and frightful barbs, but Jubilee braked, dropped her head and swerved. The top strand caught my jodhs and ripped the cloth. There came to me Nicholas's cry of, "Hi, Clare, stop!" and Bobbie's, "Oh, Clare!" and then I had lost both stirrups, and my mount and I were racing round the field for all we were worth and it seemed to me our speed was even greater than before. I was entirely out of control, and when I pulled on the reins Jubilee just stuck her head in the air and continued at her breakneck speed. I had never known her like this before and I supposed the race had turned her head. I remembered dismally that she had been fighting fit when we took her over and had had no fast work since. She was making up for it now!

Faster and faster!—and the thudding of hoofs beating in my ears. My horrified companions looking on with anxious and alarmed faces. And then another wire fence, another horrible moment and we have turned again and are galloping still round the edge of the flat stretching meadow. These are minutes I shall always remember, and throughout them I feel surprise at the great power beneath me, the length and the strength, the buoyancy of Jubilee's gallop.

It is all I can do to stay in the saddle and I abandon all hope of stopping her. I race past Bobbie, Wendy and Nicholas, and my brother shouts, "Clare, you idiot! Stop! Whoa!"

I call, "I can't! I can't!" and my voice sounds un-

*My mount and I were racing round the field for all
we were worth*

usually shrill and rather frightened. Then suddenly
Jubilee begins to slow down and I see a figure at the
gate by which we entered the field. It is a familiar
figure, holding a dark bay pony; and I realise, with a
sense of disaster, that it is Pauline.

Then Jubilee stopped and it was all over, stopped
by the gate to have a word with Firefly, whom Pauline was holding.

"Oh!" I gasped stupidly. "Oh, oh dear!"

"Whatever on earth are you doing? Are you mad?"
asked Pauline. "Galloping that mare like that. Look
at her, lathered in sweat! I shall have to write and tell
Miss Field. I can't believe she knows how little experience and horse-sense you have, otherwise she would
never have dreamt of letting you have her two jumpers. Or was she delirous when she said you could
take them over? That would explain it all."

"No, she wasn't," I said, dismounting. "She thinks we are more sensible than you do. And, after all, we do feed them properly and groom them for over an hour a day, and she knows we won't knock them about."

"But look at the tack; it's filthy!" said Pauline. "You've just polished the easy parts like the bit and stirrups and left the leather."

"We haven't!" I said, angrily. "We've spent ages on the flaps and everything."

"Well, it doesn't look like it. Miss Field will certainly rue the day she let you and Nick have her horses. Good heavens, Jubilee doesn't look as though her eyes have been sponged for a week."

I felt dangerously near tears. So much was true. I gave a sort of gulp and then I said, "I must be getting back to the others. Good-bye." And at the same moment Nicholas, Bobbie and Derek arrived on the scene.

"Thank goodness you stopped!" exclaimed Nicholas. "Oh, good afternoon, Pauline. I wondered who Clare was talking to."

"Gosh!" said Bobbie. "Didn't you go! It was wizard. How did you stay on?" Her voice was full of admiration I could not share.

"I was too afraid to fall off," I said.

"Nick, your tack! It's even worse than Clare's— *filthy*. What *would* your aunt say if she could see her horses now! Someone ought to give you two a lesson in stable management," said Pauline.

And even Nicholas was lost for words. This on top of Major Tidy's verdict was horribly convincing.

"What is it we do wrong when we tack clean, then?" I asked at last.

"I can't tell just looking now, but I expect you don't sponge all the dirt off and you put on the soap too wet—if you tack clean at all," said Pauline.

"Of course we tack clean," said Nicholas indignantly. "I'm afraid we must wend our way homewards now."

"Are you coming in or out?" asked Bobbie.

"Neither. I stopped to watch Clare's Wild West display," answered Pauline; and I felt my face slowly turning red.

"It was entirely unintentional," I said.

"You see, we were having a race," began Bobbie, "and Jubilee won, and then . . ."

"Look, we must go back or we'll be late for tea," interrupted Nicholas. Pauline moved out of the way and we filed through the gate and bade her good night.

All the way home I was silent, thinking of her words. Jubilee and her tack looked extremely dirty, and it seemed that I had failed Auntie Gay in every possible way. First we had over-fed and under-exercised her horses; then we had groomed them inefficiently, and now I had proved to all our friends and Pauline that I could not control Jubilee at all.

Nicholas tried valiantly to talk cheerfully to our guests, but his expression was false and I knew he was really feeling glum. I had muffed it again! I felt we had failed our guests too—though they were chattering gaily enough. I did not like to see two of them riding bicycles.

After we had made the horses comfortable we went indoors for tea with great appetites, and, after eating hot crumpets and strawberry jam and sandwiches, I began to feel better.

Mummy asked bright questions about our ride, and Bobbie, always talkative and sociable, told her I had won the race but did not mention the runaway act which had followed.

We all played with the dogs after tea, till Chiffon suddenly attacked Picaroon. Bobbie threw herself into the fray to help Nicholas and me part them and was bitten herself, so she had to go upstairs and have her hand bathed and bandaged.

Our guests all left in high spirits. I think they felt we had provided plenty of excitement with a runaway *and* a dogfight. And now they were glad I had not offered them a ride on Jubilee.

We saw them off down the drive, and then Nicholas turned to me and said, "The whole thing was a ghastly flop. And, of course, Pauline *would* be there."

"I'm sorry," I said.

"Oh, it wasn't your fault. I made you race and I don't expect I could have stopped her. I suppose we have done pretty badly and we've been a couple of know-alls really."

"Let's forget it for to-night," I suggested. "We might have some bright ideas to-morrow."

Dusk had fallen and the garden was grey against the darkening sky. We could hear the horses munching contentedly and we wandered indoors.

CHAPTER SEVEN

THE NEXT day Nicholas was allowed to visit Auntie Gay. The hospital is very strict about visitors and only permitted two at a time, so Mummy went with Nicholas, and I was left at home.

We had ridden quietly on the roads during the morning in wet weather and had not discussed our adventure of the day before, but Pauline's remarks about the state of our tack were still fresh in my mind, and, left on my own, I decided to pocket my pride and go down to the riding school. After all, I thought, their

C

tack always does look clean, and although Pauline is supposed to have no qualifications and is, in Auntie Gay's eyes, a poor horse-woman, that does not mean she is not a good tack cleaner.

The riding school was a scene of activity; a lesson was just about to begin, and ten children were in the act of mounting ponies in the yard. Wendy and Bobbie were helping two of them up. The tack did not look particularly clean, but I realised that it had been used in the morning and had probably just had a wipe over at lunch time. It would have its proper clean at four o'clock when the lesson had ended.

"Hallo, Clare!" called Bobbie. "What on *earth* are you doing here?"

"I've come to help," I replied rather self-consciously.

"What with?" asked Wendy.

"I want to improve my tack cleaning," I said.

"There are only three sets to clean, until after the class," Wendy told me.

"Well, I'll clean what there is if Pauline would like that and then help with the other sets later."

"Okeydoke. Come on, then," said Bobbie.

I was sorry Pauline was taking a class because I wanted her to show me how to clean tack properly. I had helped before, but everyone is in a rush at the riding school and no one had taken much notice of how I set about it. I watched Bobbie and noticed she put on less soap than me with less lather. I worked slowly and had only finished two saddles when she had done three bridles and the other saddle.

Pauline was surprised to find me there at four o'clock, and I admitted at once that I had come in the hope I could improve my tack cleaning.

"I thought if I helped you wouldn't mind telling me what I do wrong," I finished.

I must say Pauline was very nice about it and she

66

took great trouble in pointing out where it was important to rub in plenty of soap, where there was a danger of cracking and so on. She also advised me to buy a tin of Neat's Foot Oil to use when the tack had been out in the rain.

I left at five o'clock and was late home for tea.

Nicholas was so excited over his visit to Auntie Gay that he didn't wonder where I had been. He had asked her a great many questions.

"Clare, we should never have groomed Harvester and Jubilee with dandy brushes," he announced. "They are well bred and thin-skinned, and it's not so very long since they were clipped. They are not used to it—that's why poor Jubilee kicked and dug up her straw."

"What do we do when they are terribly muddy, then?" I wondered aloud.

"Oh, I asked Auntie Gay that and she said, 'sponge them,' " said Nicholas. "And you're not to ride Jubilee on such a tight rein. And they *are* to have no oats."

"We haven't any sponges," I told him.

"That's arranged, too. Auntie Gay has a couple in her saddle-room, and Mummy's going to run us over to fetch them, and we are going to bike back, and if you dare to let Stephen lose his chain I'll never forgive you," said Nicholas. "But there's one really exciting thing Auntie Gay told me. There's a Pony Club Show in ten days' time—you know, the usual annual event—and she pointed out a class to me for the Best Turned-Out Horse or Pony. The entry must have been groomed and fed, etc., by the exhibitor for not less than the last fortnight, so we can qualify."

"But how marvellous!" I said. "Of course, we won't win anything, but it will be great fun."

"No, we won't get first; we are much too inexperienced, but if we work really hard there's no reason why we shouldn't be in the running. Auntie Gay said

67

we would stand a jolly good chance if we really tried hard," said Nicholas.

"I've been down at the riding school taking a lesson in tack cleaning," I told him.

"You *haven't* . . . not really?"

"Yes, honestly, and Pauline was very nice and I've learned a lot. Did you ask about Harvester's cramp and tell her about Jubilee and the pigs?"

"Auntie Gay, you mean? Yes everything. And she was looking frightfully well, considering the awful operation," said Nicholas.

We continued to talk about Auntie Gay for some time, and then I rang up the district commissioner of our branch of the Pony Club and asked her to send me a schedule of the show. She told me we had left it rather late and if we wanted to enter for anything now it would be double entry fees. I said we definitely wanted to enter two horses for the Best Turned-Out Horse Class and would send the money when we had the schedule and would not mind the double entry fees.

Then Nicholas and I settled the horses for the night and took the tack into our play-house which had electric light, and cleaned it all again. I told Nicholas about the Neat's Foot Oil and he said that Auntie Gay had said just the same and we were to fetch a tin from her saddle-room when we went for the sponges. "In fact," finished Nicholas, "I've made a list of all the things we need and haven't got."

I won't describe our journey to Cherry Tree Cottage and back the next morning. Stephen's chain *did* come off and, although I haughtily told Nicholas I could put it on myself with the greatest of ease, I failed dismally and he had to bike a mile back again to rescue me and mend it himself. I hate bicycles and if only I had a pony of my own I would sell Stephen at once with a glad heart.

We spent the afternoon riding the horses quietly in the field on a loose rein and then grooming them. Jubilee was much quieter now I worked mostly with the body brush, though she still objected to the wisp. After tea we concentrated on the tack again, and in the evening I brushed my best riding coat and steamed my crash cap, because I was sure the rider must be especially well turned out too.

The schedule arrived the next morning and we read that we would only be expected to walk, trot and canter once round the ring on either rein.

"That's why Auntie Gay said it would be a suitable class. She knew we might have difficulty in riding Harvester and Jubilee, I expect, if there were figures of eight or anything complicated," I said.

"I think I could manage Harvester, though, now," said Nicholas.

We hacked the horses quietly on the roads and through the woods for two hours the next day, and then practised walking, trotting and cantering, one behind the other, round the field. I was becoming accustomed to the bounciness of Jubilee at last and it seemed easier now to canter on a reasonably loose rein. Nicholas seemed to manage Harvester with ease, though I thought they both looked a little wild at times.

Then, on the following day, a minor catastrophe occurred. We were cantering slowly up a grassy cart-track, which climbed steeply to the crown of the rough, sparse hill, when Harvester put one of his great hoofs into a rabbit hole and turned a somersault. For a terrible moment I thought he had broken his neck and then he gave a grunt and started to move, and I thought it must be a leg which was damaged. Meanwhile, Nicholas had fallen clear and quickly jumped to his feet. He made a quick rush at Harvester, meaning to grab the rein, but he only succeeded in frightening the horse so that he scrambled up and trotted away.

"Oh, Christmas! What on earth happened? I've got the dickens of a stiff neck already and my arm hurts a bit," said Nicholas.

But I had seen he was not badly hurt and I was thinking now of Harvester, who was trotting away into the distance with trailing reins. He looked rather magnificent, handsome, noble and forlorn, like a charger who has lost his rider in battle. I saw him tread on a rein and break it, and then I saw him tread on the end which wasn't broken and stop dead and throw up his head because he had jerked his own mouth.

Then I started slowly in pursuit, calling, "Whoa, Harvester, steady!"

To my joy he turned and trotted back towards me; and he wasn't lame, though he had a graze on the near knee. His dear handsome forehead was covered in sticky mud and he had broken his bridle in four places, so the bit was hanging out of his mouth and the reins were useless.

I caught him easily and Nicholas groaned when he saw the extent of the damage, though the graze was nothing to worry about. Jubilee only had one pair of reins, so I could not lend Harvester any part of her bridle. We eventually decided that Nicholas should ride home and I should lead his mount by the noseband. Our horses seemed quiet now, almost sleepy. We walked all the way home and arrived just in time for lunch.

Nicholas was rather down-hearted. He had spent hours getting the bridle supple with glistening buckles. "If I go and buy a new one it will be all horribly stiff. I shall never get it looking really nice in time for the show," he lamented.

Then I suddenly realised that Auntie Gay must have

a spare bridle stored away. A well-known show rider must have spare tack, in case of emergencies. I suggested Nicholas should bike over and search the tackroom at Cherry Tree Cottage. Auntie Gay never keeps anything locked up, so he could search all the cupboards and the big box.

When we were home again we bathed Harvester's knee and dusted it with powder. He was very solemn, stood beautifully still and made no fuss at all.

After lunch Nicholas followed my suggestion and biked over to Cherry Tree Cottage, where he discovered two complete spare bridles, a spare saddle, two additional pairs of reins and various bits and pieces, and I took the dogs for a long walk.

I was afraid we had neglected them rather of late and they were certainly overjoyed to find I was taking them out again at last. Chiffon and Picaroon had a fight on the way home, but Gambler was an angel and kept by me the whole time.

I felt sure Picaroon was missing Auntie Gay and I was rather haunted by remorse to think we had devoted so much time to the horses and so little to dog and cat, though Luke had settled down in the kitchen and seemed devoted to Mrs. Tubb, who adored him.

Nicholas and I spent the evening cleaning tack and grooming the horses.

The next day we both had to spend most of the morning at the dentist, which was infuriating. We schooled the horses all afternoon, groomed them until dusk had darkened into night and then cleaned tack in our play-house until Daddy appeared in anger and asked us whether we were aware the time was ten o'clock.

Nicholas put a tremendous amount of elbow grease into the bridle he had fetched the day before. It was fairly supple because it had been well oiled when put away in store. I slept the dreamless sleep of the physically weary that night.

The next day we spent the whole morning trying to teach ourselves how to plait manes, for Auntie Gay insisted that for a Best Turned-Out Class the entries must have plaited manes. Jubilee was used to jumping with hers loose and she did not like my amateurish attempt to sew it in neat plaits. Harvester was as obliging as ever, but Nicholas is a poor sewer and he pricked one of his fingers, and it bled on the neat strands of mane and reddened his shirt.

I said I would go to the riding school and ask Pauline to give me a lesson, but Nicholas said it wasn't necessary; we must learn by bitter experience and long, hard work. I said why should the horses suffer, because we were too conceited to take lessons? And he said Harvester wasn't suffering but enjoying all the attention. We were becoming angry with one another when, as twelve struck, the baker's man appeared on the scene. He stopped to talk to the horses and then laughed when he saw Nicholas's untidy attempts at plaiting.

"Never see such a mess, not in all my life," he said. "Call that plaiting? Move out of the way and I'll show you how it *should* be done."

He picked up Auntie Gay's scissors and cut out the thread Nicholas had so painfully sewn in a few moments before. "Now, look. *This* is the way to do it. But you must damp the mane well first, like this. Now part off the six locks that are going to be plaits, see—you must get a good clean parting, no wispy bits. Didn't you know I used to be a groom—ar, but that was a long way back in the 'twenties before you were born. Rode second horseman for old Colonel Harper, I did, and *he* had a fine stable too."

He rambled on and we watched his busy, efficient fingers. Harvester stood still and contented, his head in the sunshine.

"Wonderful old horse this, wonderful, better than that skittish little mare, though she's got a jump in her all right—saw them both at Latfield Show last summer. Real sad about Miss Field," he continued.

Nicholas explained about the Pony Club Show, and he said if we needed any help any time we were to let him know and then, having put up Harvester's mane at miraculous speed in twenty-five minutes, he said he had better be getting on with the delivering or someone would be creating for sure.

He left whistling gaily, and Nicholas and I gazed in wonder at the six neat plaits.

Then it was lunch-time. In the late afternoon I managed to put up the whole of Jubilee's mane. It looked wispy and uneven when I had finished, but at least I had sewn seven pleats, including a forelock, of a sort. But then an awful thing happened. Jubilee became exasperated by my fumbling and she would not let me cut them out. She reared whenever I touched her mane, and at last I had to give in.

"It will ruin her mane, but she'll just have to sleep in them for the night now," I told Nicholas. "She's bumped my nose three times and I'm worn out and fed up."

In the morning next day she was calm and I took them out without much difficulty.

CHAPTER EIGHT

THE DAY of the Pony Club Show dawned bright and clear. The dew-wet grass sparkled in the morning sunshine and the young leaves were touched with gold. Our class was the first and started at ten o'clock, so we rose at half-past five.

Jubilee had lain in a dirty part of her stable during the night and had several stable stains, so I started by washing most of her, and particularly her tail, with soap-suds, and then rinsing her with blue bag and lukewarm water. She hates being washed and soon became impatient. She danced from side to side and kicked the bucket over, which made her straw wet and sodden. When I had dried her, I gave her a hay-net and then I mucked out the stable.

Jubilee seemed to know this was a special day and she was too excited to eat much. She pulled the hay out of the net in large hasty mouthfuls and then let half of it fall on the floor.

When I had finished the stable and picked out her hoofs, I led her round the drive several times, hoping the sun would finish drying her coat. Then I started to groom her with a body brush. Nicholas was well ahead of me, as Harvester did not need washing, and he had started to plait. Every now and then an "Ow!" told me he had pricked his finger.

Presently I started to work on Jubilee's mane with a damp brush, which she did not enjoy. She tossed her head from side to side, and I felt sure she thought I was being very tiresome and plaiting was quite un-

74

necessary. After all, Auntie Gay never plaited her mane for shows, not even for the White City!

It was breakfast time when I had finished the first two plaits and I was in a predicament, because I was afraid to leave Jubilee tied up, for fear that she might put a foot over her head-collar rope and break her leg; yet, if I left her untied she would probably rub out her plaits and break more hairs in her mane. In the end I decided: better risk the mane than the leg, and I left her loose in the box and hurried indoors.

It was Wednesday so breakfast was at the usual week-day hour of eight o'clock. I gobbled like mad and Daddy said I would have acute indigestion and Mummy said I would have gastric ulcers in later life as a result of always rushing my food.

Time was growing short because we had planned to leave at nine o'clock, and I soon grew desperate as I struggled again with Jubilee's fine and wispy mane. Nicholas had finished plaiting Harvester, who, to my surprise, looked very tidy and well groomed, and, at last, he offered to help me.

"I'll do the forelock," he offered. "Come on, hand over the grey thread."

He was very brisk, but he pricked his thumb again and spattered Jubilee's clean grey coat with blood. I went away to fetch a damp sponge to repair the damage, and when I returned I found Nicholas finishing the last plait for me.

"Thanks awfully, but do you think it's strictly fair —I mean, oughtn't I to have done it?" I asked dubiously.

"What a ghastly sentence! 'Oughtn't I'!" exclaimed Nicholas, handing me the needle and thread. "I thought all girls could sew. I shouldn't fuss about the fairness side of it: we are certainly not likely to win anything unless there's a booby prize."

75

I polished Jubilee with the rubber, sponged her nostrils and oiled her neat, well-shaped hoofs, and then I simply dashed indoors to change.

We were only ten minutes behind schedule when we left and the horses seemed glad to be out and on their way. They walked with long swinging strides, as though they knew they were not just out for an everyday hack.

"I wonder if they think they are about to enter for a jumping competition," mused Nicholas. "But, of course, Auntie Gay generally takes them by horsebox."

"They must be filled with trepidation if they think *we* are going to jump them," I said.

The showground was already crowded when we arrived at ten minutes to ten, and the first thing which met our eyes was a fair-haired girl with her sleeves rolled up, energetically polishing a golden chestnut with a rubber.

"She'll win," declared Nicholas. "Look at the shine on that pony's coat!"

"Mummy's not here with our hoof oil and grooming kit yet, and we've only ten minutes and Jubilee's sweating," I said.

"We must get our numbers at once. Come on, there's the Secretary's Tent, hurry," called Nicholas, breaking into a canter.

Jubilee was very, very excited. She looked round the ring, which was dotted with jumps, as though she was already planning exactly how she would behave.

We met Bobbie and Tinkerbell. "Hallo! Your horses do look posh, absolutely wizard, honestly!" she said.

"Thank you. I don't think they look too good, though," I said. "My plaits are awful."

"What about mine, then?" asked Bobbie.

"Well, we won't be the worst in the class, anyway. Tinkerbell's a jolly sight dirtier than our mounts," whispered Nicholas, as we moved on towards the Secretary's Tent.

Wendy was there, collecting her number too. "Hallo! What are you entering for?" she asked in bright accents. We told her, and she said. "Oh, so that is why you came for tack-cleaning instruction, Clare," and she laughed a little derisively. "You should have heard what Pauline had to say about the state of your tack and your riding after she saw you galloping round that field—golly!"

"I think I can guess. It was pretty filthy and we shall probably be stuck in the back row to-day. But Clare went round to the riding school *before* she knew about the Best Turned-Out Class, actually," said Nicholas.

We rode away and found Mummy and spent a hasty seven minutes polishing the horses and their tack. Luckily the class started a little late and ten struck before we were called in the collecting ring.

I felt awful and slightly sick. Nicholas talked a great deal to everyone, which I knew meant he was feeling awful too. I always become deadly silent with the needle, but he always becomes madly talkative and quite inconsequential.

At last we were told by a loud-speaker to enter the ring. Jubilee had her eyes on the jumps and I could feel her trembling with excitement. She was full of impulsion and walked with a wonderful cadence. I remembered Auntie Gay telling me that Jubilee was always highly nervous and tense before jumping a round, whereas Harvester was calm, cool and sensible. But then their styles of jumping were entirely different. Jubilee was like a flying machine and as nimble and agile as a cat, and Harvester would jump round

77

a ring with an easy cadence, no dash, no rush, no excitement. I often marvelled at the way Auntie Gay could manage two horses with such entirely different temperaments so successfully.

The fair-haired girl led the way on her chestnut pony, which shone like polished gold. His plaits were neat and even. Nicholas followed her and I followed Nicholas. Bobbie was behind me and she called, "I say. Fancy having six plaits, Clare! It's unlucky. You *must* have uneven numbers—seven or nine."

I didn't answer. I watched Harvester's tail and tried to keep a length away. Soon a tall lank judge in rat-catcher and Army field boots told us to trot, and, a few moments later, to canter. Sunshine glinted and played on our bits and stirrups; the breeze, laced with the smell of warm earth, trampled grass, horse-flesh and leather, blew softly against our cheeks. A small crowd of people watched us at the ringside.

Soon we were told to change the rein. Jubilee was growing excited and, every now and then, she glanced at the jump.

We all broke back into a trot, crossed the ring diagonally and cantered again; and it was as we reached the far corner of the ring that a minor catastrophe occurred. Suddenly Jubilee snatched at the reins, swerved to the left and lengthened her stride. Harvester's large elegant liver chestnut tail was no longer ahead of me, but in its place was a white five-barred gate with two large wings. I had been riding on a fairly loose rein and it seemed to me too late for any action on my part now. The gate loomed before me. I grabbed hold of Jubilee's third plait with both hands and hoped wildly for the best; she lengthened her stride again, dropped her head a little and then took off. For one superb moment we were in mid-air and then we were coming down to earth again and I

78

had lost both my stirrups. . . . "I haven't fallen off!" I though with amazement. . . . "I'm still here."

I caught a glimpse of Derek and Dick standing at the ringside. I heard a muttered, "She's showing off!" and then we had reached another corner and I realised we would soon be approaching another jump. This time I stopped Jubilee in time and we cantered gaily past a substantial black brush fence.

Then I noticed all the other riders were being called into the centre. Nicholas said afterwards that he thought I had alarmed the judges so much by my obvious lack of control that they thought it would be safest to bring everyone to a standstill as soon as possible.

I pulled up to a walk and felt myself growing red in the face, and then a rather hard-faced woman wearing a Melton cloth hunting coat, felt hat and well-cut breeches and boots told me to join the other competitors. There were twelve of us and we stood in a long line. The girl on the chestnut was at the top and then a fat girl with a stout, black cob, and then Nicholas and Harvester. I was at the bottom and I noticed that I had pulled one of Jubilee's plaits out.

"Poor old girl; she thinks she's meant to jump. How is Miss Field, by the way?" said the judge in ratcatcher, kindly patting Jubilee's neck.

I told him Auntie Gay was much better, thank you, and then he joined the hard-faced lady, and they started to inspect all the entries—starting at the top.

Each rider had to dismount, unsaddle his horse and stand him up properly while the judges looked at the tack, ran their hands through the horses' coats and felt their legs and muscles.

At last they reached me, and Jubilee was very good. She stood beautifully and gazed with dark brilliant eyes towards the triple bar. But there was dust beneath

For one superb moment we were in mid-air

her saddle, and I wished I had oiled her feet again before entering the ring.

"She jumped that gate splendidly," said the lady judge.

"I think you two are very sporting to look after Miss Field's horses while she is in hospital, very sporting indeed," said the judge in rat-catcher, running his hand down Jubilee's hard, short tendons. "Lovely clean legs this mare has, too."

"I think we are jolly lucky to have the chance, though I'm dreadfully sorry about Auntie Gay. I mean, it *is* awful," I muttered belatedly, forgetting the many times Mummy had told me *not* to mutter.

"The inside of your noseband is not all that could be desired and you've lost a plait, which is a pity," said the hard-faced lady.

"The buckles need more spit and polish, but the mare's clean all right—nice coat she's got," said the judge in rat-catcher.

"Thank you," I muttered, and I saw Nicholas, at the far end of the line, making a face at me which meant: speak up and don't look glum.

The judges moved away and went into conference. I looked at Harvester, shining like burnished copper in the sun, and the cob, black and hard as ebony, and the golden chestnut with his neat plaits and sparkling white star.

Then Bobbie called, "Clare! Did you think it was a jumping class?"

I said "No," and started to replace Jubilee's saddle.

Out of the corner of my eye, I saw a steward handing rosettes to the hard-faced lady. A moment later the red was given to the fair-haired girl and her chestnut gelding. Someone clapped: the judges offered their congratulations and passed on to the fat girl and cob, who were given the blue for a second. And a moment later Nicholas was handed a yellow rosette for third. Then the judges paused for a moment, hovering by Wendy and Dawn and a little curly-headed boy with a Dartmoor pony. I gave Nicholas a long glance which meant jolly good, cheers! And when I had finished the judges had handed Wendy a green rosette and then, to my surprise, I realised they were approaching me.

"And you have a very highly commended," said the judge in rat-catcher. "Your horse is in very good condition, but your tack doesn't quite make the grade. Pity about the plait, too. Never mind, jolly sporting effort."

Determined not to mutter, I said, "Oh, thank you, thank you very much," and I spoke so loudly everyone at the ringside heard.

Then we were cantering round the ring and I had my first rosette, a pink one, in my mouth. I was following in Dawn's wake now with her grey tail waving like a flag in front of me. I heard two little boys call out, "Hi, look! There goes the cove that jumped the gate! Isn't she smashing?"

And then it was all over and Bobbie was saying, "Jolly good, you were wizard, honestly," and Mummy was saying, "Well done. I never thought you would win anything. Gay *will* be pleased."

"No one is more surprised than me," declared Nicholas. "I think Harvester must have mesmerised the judges. Of course, he definitely is the winning type."

We stayed for a while, watching the equitation class and the junior jumping class, and letting our horses graze in head-collars. Then, as we had no stable for them and dared not tie them up as they were not used to it, we started for home.

The next afternoon we were both allowed to visit Auntie Gay. I do not like hospitals; the strong smell of antiseptic, the bare, clean walls, the bustling nurses and the doctors in their white coats all send a shiver down my spine. They seem such sterile comfortless places.

Auntie Gay was in a ward sitting up in a white iron bed with a blue counterpane and she was looking surprisingly well.

"Hallo! Sit down both of you, please. Well, how did it go off?" she asked.

We told her and she was very encouraging.

"But that's marvellous and your first attempt, too! It's wonderful . . . two more rosettes for Jubilee and Harvester," she said.

"But wasn't it awful about the jump? Everyone thought I was trying to show off," I told her.

"Poor Jubilee was only trying to do the right thing. After all, she hardly ever goes into a ring except to jump and she probably thought you were being rather dumb and half-witted, so she had better take things into her own hands—or hoofs!"

We talked solely of the show for the first half-hour, and then I suddenly realised that we had not asked Auntie Gay how she was feeling.

Then she told us that she would soon be out of hospital and that she was coming to stay with us for the whole summer with just a break of a fortnight in June, when she was going to the sea.

"But this is terrific!!" said Nicholas. "Why didn't we know before? It's wonderful."

"It wasn't fixed till the day before yesterday when your mother suggested it," said Auntie Gay.

"Will you still be ill? I mean, will you have to stay in bed all the time? Or will you be able to walk in the garden a little?" I asked, an idea forming in my mind.

"Of course I won't have to stay in bed, you goat,"

she said, laughing, "not all the time. I'm not a wheel-chair case, thank heavens, just convalescent, which means I must take it easy and not ride until the autumn at the earliest."

"And you'll have breakfast in bed every morning, I suppose, and rest after lunch and that sort of thing," added Nicholas.

"Yes, I think so. Doesn't it sound ghastly?"

"Will you be able to walk in our paddock and stand about?" I asked, fixing my eyes on the bevy of flowers on her locker and bedside table, and wishing suddenly that we had brought a bunch to add to them.

She looked at me with her very bright blue eyes and began to laugh again. "What *are* you getting at, Clare?" she asked. "Why should I want to stand about? Or, rather, why is it especially important that I should be *allowed* to stand about?"

"Oh, nothing," I said, hurriedly. The question that was in my mind seemed so momentous that I was afraid to ask because I knew I would be so bitterly disappointed if she said no.

"Are we tiring you, Auntie Gay?" asked Nicholas anxiously.

"Are we staying too long?"

"Not at all. Now, come on, Clare—out with it!"

"Well," I said, "well, you see, I wondered—no, I *can't* ask."

"She's probably wondering whether you will let the horses stay on with us. We would just love to have them, if you think we are capable, and they'll be fit to be at grass when we go back to school, won't they?" said Nicholas.

"Of course, I want you to keep them, but from now on I'm going to pay for their keep. I've discussed all this with your mother. And in the summer holidays I'm going to give you both riding lessons, so you can both manage Harvester and Jubilee beautifully and there will be no more runaway acts," said Auntie Gay.

"That's wonderful, thank you very much," said Nicholas enthusiastically.

"It's super!" I cried. "That's what I was going to ask you—if you'd give us some lessons—but I was afraid it would be too much of a beastly bore."

"No, I want to teach you and I want your jumping to improve—it's shocking!"

"Yes, I know," I admitted.

We talked about the days ahead, the jumps we would build in the paddock and the school exercises we must learn. Then the topic changed to Luke and Picaroon, and a few moments later a nurse told us it was time to go: Miss Field must not be tired.

Nicholas jumped guiltily to his feet but Auntie Gay said, "Don't dash off! I've something for each of you." She pointed to two large, rather flat brown-paper parcels between the locker and wall. "Can you see them? Don't unpack them here. Look at them in the car. Carry them carefully, they're breakable."

Nicholas lifted out the two parcels gently, saying, "You shouldn't have done it. We love looking after the horses. They've made these holidays the best we've ever had."

"It's been wizard," I said inadequately.

The brisk, neat nurse came bustling back. "I'm sorry," she said, "but I must ask you to go at once; the visiting times to-day are two-thirty till four. We can't make exceptions."

"Go on, hurry, but don't drop the parcels. Good-bye, and thank you for the visit and for looking after the horses," said Auntie Gay.

I looked at her as she settled back against the pillows; and she was not wan or grey-faced as I had expected to see her, nor had she the hectic flush which

85

I had imagined as an alternative during our drive to the hospital. But she looked very like the usual Auntie Gay with her hair still short and curly, her cheeks glowing and the familiar smile turning up the corners of her mouth. Only her eyes seemed to betray her and show signs of illness; they were very bright and there were dark shadows beneath them, which gave her an unusually fragile appearance.

We waved to her as we left the ward and then walked in silence down the long corridor and out into the sunlight.

"She's looking marvellous," said Nicholas.

"Hardly ill at all," I added.

"You wouldn't think she was not long off the danger list. I hope we didn't stay too long. Jolly decent of her to say she would give us jumping lessons. It's going to be wizard, you know. We'll get really first class if we concentrate on it," continued Nicholas.

"And these presents, too. I wonder what's in them," I said.

Mummy was waiting at the hospital gates; we rushed into the car and started to untie the string of the parcels.

"Did you choose these for Auntie Gay, Mummy?" asked Nicholas, searching his pockets for a knife.

"Not exactly, though I fetched them. Come on, Clare, let me open it—all your fingers are thumbs."

"I'm so excited," I said.

At last I was unwrapping the brown paper and inside was a wonderful picture by Cecil Aldin of a meet of hounds outside an inn called The Crooked Billet. Right in the foreground was a grey horse with a dark mane and tail.

"Oh, how super," I cried. "Look! I shall hang it above my bed. Isn't the grey horse just like Jubilee?"

Then I saw a little note which had fallen to the car

floor. Picking it up, I read, "Clare, with love and thanks from Auntie Gay, Jubilee, Picaroon and Luke."

"The picture is an original, not a reproduction, so be careful with it," said Mummy. "Let's see yours, Nicholas."

He showed us his sporting print of a hunt in full cry, and the little note, which accompanied it and was the same as mine, except Harvester's name was in the place of Jubilee's.

"It's marvellous! I shall take it back to school with me and when I have a study it will hang there in honour above the fireplace," he told us.

All the way home we talked of the future. I felt my dreams had come true. Harvester and Jubilee were not going back; they would stay with us all the summer! Auntie Gay, who had jumped for England, would teach us to ride them and she would be with us all the long summer holidays.

I had longed for her to be well again and yet dreaded the wrench of parting with Jubilee. But now the days ahead were full of promise and I looked at my picture again and felt this was the happiest moment of my life.

"And tomorrow," said Nicholas," we must start building those jumps. . . ."

Friends Must Part

CHAPTER ONE

W E LIVE at Springfield Farm; our meadows are green and damp most of the year round, like fields in spring; the river winds slowly through our rich and tranquil valley, and our pasture is known to be the best for many miles.

Daddy is a dairy-farmer and we have a pedigree herd of soft-eyed Jersey cows and two hefty dark bulls, called Springtime Chevalier and Springtime Sorcerer. I have two favourite cows, which are very tame and fond of sugar, and their names are Limelight and Evensong.

My brothers, Ian and Rodney, are eight and ten years old when this story begins; and I am twelve. They are both fond of bicycles, trains and children's thrillers, but Daddy wishes they were fond of cows and farming.

Our house is a fairly large red brick farm-house with a tiled roof and sash windows. It is supposed to have been built about one hundred and fifty years ago, and Mummy says it is very inconvenient to run; dust rises from the floors, as if by magic, at all hours of the day; the passages are long and cold and the bathroom is enormous. The spacious kitchen with a lovely large uneconomical range has a giant dresser which is always littered with colic drinks, odd bottles of antiseptic, screws, nails and many other odds and ends.

But although Mummy often complains about the

haphazard planning of the house, she prefers it to the neat, modernised cottage opposite, which is described by the local house agent as: *This Lovely Gem. A Charming Thatched Old World Cottage Residence with 3 bedrooms, bathroom, 2 reception rooms, kitchenette and attractive entrance hall. Garage. Delightful Garden. Paddock. In all 2 Acres.*

It was here, ten years after my parents bought Springfield Farm, that Harriet Kingsley came to live. The name was changed from Sweet Briar Cottage to the original unassuming Nut Tree Cottage. New, bright, handprinted curtains decorated the windows; elaborate changes were made in the garden and, most exciting of all, a portable loose-box arrived.

Of course I'm mad on riding and ponies; and, at that time, I still had my first pony, my dear milk-white Peppermint. He was over twenty then and had gone in the wind, but he was very willing and, not being particularly well trained, he always wanted to gallop as soon as he felt turf beneath his feet, and, as he was broken-winded, this made some of our rides rather difficult. We have no farm horses and I had long been afraid that Peppermint might be lonely with only cows for company. Now, I thought, eyeing the loose-box, he's going to have a friend opposite.

I saw Harriet two days after the Kingsleys had moved in. I was up early because I wanted to see Evensong's calf, which had been born during the night. Harriet was up early to see the sun rise behind the gentle wooded slope beyond the silver winding river; to see the damp and dewy fields brighten and sparkle in the morning sunlight; and to see and hear an unfamiliar countryside welcome the coming of another summer day. The slow cows came mooing over the meadow to be milked in the long airy cow-sheds; the chickens rushed from their houses with a wild

89

flapping of wings to gobble the pale oats George had thrown for them. Two bright-coloured birds bathed in a little puddle by our front door, and over in the field beyond our lawn Peppermint lay dozing in the long grass.

I saw Harriet from my window as she stood at her garden gate, a fair neat figure in grey pleated shorts, an aertex shirt and sandals. She did not look tough, but she looked nice and she looked friendly. I remembered the loose-box. . . . She *must* be horsey. Suddenly I wondered if she would like to see Evensong's calf. Blondie, our Boxer bitch, ran ahead of me, as I ran downstairs, and, always madly sociable, welcomed Harriet to the neighbourhood before I had spoken one word.

"What a lovely dog. Is she yours?" said Harriet, when she had recovered from the effusive onslaught.

"Well, she belongs to all of us, really. Her name's Blondie. Mine's Andy—Andy Fairfax—and I'm wondering if you would like to see our new calf; she was only born last night—that's why I'm up extra early this morning. Her mother's Evensong and she's Evensong's ninth calf."

"Oh, how wizard! I should love to. My name's Harriet, but I expect you know that. Mummy says the whole village knew all about us long before we arrived. Somebody's aunt knew somebody who worked for Daddy in the year two," she said, twiddling Blondie's ears. "What's your grey pony called? Daddy's going to buy me a pony soon."

We wandered round to one of the calving boxes and fed Evensong on apples and looked at the little warm brown calf lying snugly in the deep straw. I discovered Harriet was to be a day girl at my school, St. Catherine's. I discovered she loved riding, drawing and reading and, like myself, collected pony books.

From that day onwards we were friends. In term-time we caught the bus to school together and we sat next to each other in class. We helped each other with our prep and swopped all information. Harriet's maths were hopeless, but her English, French and Latin were excellent. My maths were passable, my English and Latin about average and my French atrocious, so we both gained from the arrangement. Our form was a fairly large one with twenty-six children, and before Harriet came I had belonged to a gang of five of us who always went round together: Muriel, Jill, Susan, Bobs and I. For some reason Muriel took an instant dislike to Harriet, and so I gradually drifted apart from the gang and Harriet and I just went round together.

At the week-ends and in the holidays Harriet and I used to take it in turns to ride Peppermint. We would go for long expeditions, one walking, the other riding, and Blondie always accompanied us. Harriet liked Blondie so much that the Kingsleys bought a Boxer puppy themselves; she was christened Sheba and I helped to teach her to come when she was called, shake hands and die for her country.

Of course we had many disagreements and quarrels. Harriet was always slow to dress in the mornings and was generally late for everything, which often made me furious. She used to catch the bus by the skin of her teeth each morning. Sometimes we would agree to start on one of our expeditions at two o'clock and she wouldn't be ready till half-past. Once I went without her.

But Harriet was awfully difficult to quarrel with in those days. She just said, "I know and I'm sorry. I can't help it, so do shut up." And she never took me very seriously. Yet in the end our quarrel started in such a trivial way.

We would go for long expeditions.

It was autumn, one of those muggy days when the
air seems thick and heavy and people's tempers are
frayed. The morning had started badly for me, because Mummy had told me at breakfast that I was to
tidy up my bedroom. I gave a deep sigh, because I had
wanted to wash Peppermint's mane and tail before the
long ride which Harriet and I had planned to take together in the afternoon. Daddy told me it was rude to
sigh like that and if I couldn't be civil at breakfast I
had better go back to bed. Unlike Harriet, I am not a
tidy person and it took me an hour to make my room
respectable and, of course, I broke my tooth mug and
had to spend ages crawling around and picking up the
bits. Then I lost my hair-grip and upset the dustpan I
had just filled, while looking for the hair-grip.

I managed to start washing Peppermint's mane and
tail at eleven, and then Mrs. Biggs, who washes up for

us and peels the vegetables, called to me to come in for elevenses. Mummy insists on my having a glass of milk at eleven every morning when I am at home, so I had to leave Peppermint.

Mrs. Biggs had run out of onions and wanted a cabbage, so she said, "Just run down to the shop and get them for me, Andy—there's a duck."

I saw my morning disappearing and Peppermint half-wet in the stable.

"Oh, no! Not again, Biggie, please. Can't we have something else?"

"Now look, Andy Fairfax," said Mrs. Biggs in the firm tone she assumes on these occasions, "I've got a nice bit of steak to cook for your lunch to-day and you can't 'ave steak without onions. If you won't go I shall 'ave to ask your mother and she's busy with them agricultural forms for your father."

"All right, all right. I'll go," I said, feeling I had been a perfect pig. When I returned from the shop I found Peppermint had got out of his stable and had a roll. His white coat was covered with mud and his wet tail was dark and bedraggled. He looked very old and very disreputable, but his eyes were bright and shining. He was in a naughty mood and had no intention of suffering any more washing. It was lunch-time when I had succeeded in catching him.

I gobbled my steak and onions, but my parents ate very slowly so I had to wait for them. I offered to wash up the dishes instead of drying them as I usually do, because I thought I could get out to the stable more quickly, but, of course, I broke a plate in my haste and Mummy told me I was becoming a very clumsy child, and then I cut my hand on a broken and ragged piece of plate and dripped blood on my new riding shirt. It was two o'clock by the time I reached the stable again and we had decided to start at two.

Peppermint was dry again now and the mud came off fairly easily with a dandy brush. I worked so fast I grew very hot and cross. I wished Harriet had not had an appointment at the dentist's in the morning. She should have been helping me to groom Peppermint, I thought, as I started to brush his muddy tail. It was important that we should start by two o'clock, because we had planned to explore a new way through deep fir woods and across a stretch of downland, and we wanted to get home again before dark. It's just like her to be late to-day, of all days, I thought unreasonably; and I remembered all the other days she had been late, all the times I had waited in the stable-yard for her. I ran and fetched the saddle and one of the stirrups slipped and hit me a sharp blow on my thigh.

I cried, "Oh!" and Blondie, bursting with sympathy, nearly sent me flying headlong in her excitement. The animals, Mrs. Biggs, the tooth glass and the plate all seemed against me and helped to make my temper worse. I felt like sitting down and crying with sheer exasperation.

I saddled Peppermint and he nipped me when I tightened the girths, but I didn't scold him because he had done it for years and was too old to be scolded now. I looked at my watch. It was a quarter-past two. I thought of Harriet dawdling through her lunch while I dashed to and fro in mad haste to be ready by two o'clock. Late again, I thought, rubbing my thigh. Then suddenly I felt furious. Why should I hang about waiting for Harriet?

Normally I would go round to Nut Tree Cottage and rout her out, but now I decided on the spur of the moment to go without her. After all, she knew the ride would be spoilt if we could not get away by two o'clock.

I bridled Peppermint, called Blondie and mounted.

Then feeling hot, dirty and angry. I rode away down the drive. Peppermint, glad to be off, walked with a brisk, springy step and cocked ears. I felt my temper subsiding a little, but I was still determined to go without Harriet. Anyway, I told myself, Mrs. Kingsley would not have liked me to barge into their lunch, and I'm jolly well not going to shout my head off in the road.

It was half-past two now, so I decided to go a shorter ride than the one we had planned. I turned off to the left and took the grassy track which leads to Brazely Common. The bracken was turning a beautiful brown, the heather was still in bloom and the beech leaves were gold and copper, for autumn had come early this year. The hedges and the grass had lost their greenness and the gorse bushes were dull and brittle. Blondie hunted, giving tongue and darting here, there and everywhere.

I wondered whether Harriet was looking for me and realised I should have left a message with my parents or one of the farm-hands to say that I had started without her. I cantered on a stretch of grass between pines; the warm breeze was in my face and brought the warm old scents of autumn. If Harriet had been here she would probably have quoted from the *Ode to Autumn* and I began to miss her company. She would probably have been calling, "Wait, wait," too, I reflected.

Somehow I didn't enjoy my ride as much as usual and that made me feel all the angrier with Harriet. When on returning I found her calmly sitting on her garden gate and swinging her legs I felt furious.

Blondie ran forward to greet Sheba with her usual good manners, but I called angrily, "I'm tired of waiting for you day after day. You spoilt our lovely long ride and everything."

"I was only ten minutes late and I couldn't help it,"

95

said Harriet. "You knew I had to go to the dentist I think you played a dirty trick, but actually, as it happens, I couldn't care less." She spoke with a calmness which infuriated me.

"All right," I said, "if you couldn't care less, don't come any more. I don't care. I'm just as happy on my own—in fact, happier. I don't have to do so much walking. Next time you want a ride ask someone else."

I saw Harriet turn scarlet and for a moment I regretted my words: then she said with dignity, "Right, I will remember that," and, jumping off the gate, she walked stiffly into Nut Tree Cottage and shut the door.

Something about her face told me she was really offended, much more so than myself. My anger would subside in an hour or two, but she would not forget my words for many a day.

I turned Peppermint out in the field near our house and gave him a feed before wandering indoors and laying tea. "Where was Harriet this afternoon?" asked Mummy.

"She didn't turn up, so I went without her," I said shortly.

"I saw her hanging around the stable looking very disconsolate at about three and I wondered what on earth had happened," Mummy told me.

Suddenly I felt haunted by remorse, but the next moment I told myself the whole affair was Harriet's fault, not mine. If she hadn't been late we would never have quarrelled.

Ian came running into the room, interrupting my thoughts. "Oh, goody—cream buns! Rod! Rod! Cream buns! Hurry up, slow coach," he called.

"Help Andy make the tea, and don't make so much noise," said Mummy.

"Why did you go without Harriet, Andy?" asked Rodney.

96

"That's my affair," I said angrily. "Why don't you fetch the cake and lend a hand?"

"Oh, who would have an elder sister?" wailed Rodney. "They are all the same. Do this, do that."

CHAPTER TWO

NEXT MORNING Harriet missed the bus to school and, wondering whether she was ill, I felt a wave of remorse. It was Monday and everyone was talking about the week-end.

Bobs called, "Where's Harriet, Andy? Is she ill?"

I felt awkward; I did not want to admit we had quarrelled and I thought we might possibly make it up before the gang found out.

"I don't know," I answered cautiously. "I expected her to be on the bus as usual. Probably she overslept; she never has a moment to spare in the mornings, anyway."

"I saw her yesterday," said Muriel, "just after tea. She was in a temper. I asked what was eating her and she said you were a false friend, and a lot of other things besides."

I felt myself growing hot. . . . *A false friend*—what greater insult could there be? I started to empty my satchel without a word.

"Did you have a row or something?" asked Susan in a small voice. I could not trust myself to answer. I couldn't bear them to hear a quaver in my voice.

"Not half," said Muriel, "judging from Harriet."

"Can't you make it up?" said Bobs. "Is it so very awful?"

I hated them for their curiosity and I hated Harriet for letting me down. I twisted my bungi in my hand

and said, "Oh, shut up!" And then, luckily, it was time for prayers.

Harriet arrived at half-past nine and cut me dead, sticking her short straight nose in the air as she hurried by.

From that day onwards we were open enemies. My parents were furious they said we were both being very stupid and making mountains out of mole-hills, allowing some trivial incident, a few hasty words, to assume such proportions.

I missed Harriet at the week-ends, which made me dislike her the more. She soon had her desk moved away from mine next to a Swedish girl, called Pauline. I became a member of the gang once more and Muriel would tell me just what Harriet thought of me. When Harriet and I had to contact each other we sent messages through a third person.

It is difficult to live opposite somebody, with whom you have quarrelled, especially when you have been great friends. Once I met Harriet face to face in the road and said, "I say, isn't it a super day"—one of those silly things one says on an embarrassing occasion —but she ignored me.

The dogs were tactless. *They* were still friends whatever their owners might think, and whenever they met they gave each other that effusive welcome which only Boxers can give. Sheba had always loved our garden and would often turn up by the front door in search of Blondie, and now we had quarrelled she had no intention of giving up this habit.

Harriet sometimes had to creep around our house in search of Sheba. She was always very polite to my parents, but ignored me. I had never realised she was such a determined character nor capable of so long a silence until then, and it seemed to me I had discovered a new and nasty side to Harriet.

Of course I never spoke to her again after my one attempt in the road and, though I often felt we had made a very large mountain out of a minute molehill, I now considered her a false friend too.

The months flew by and autumn turned to winter. The trees, bare and naked of leaves, creaked and groaned in the November winds; the fields were wet and muddy underfoot: and day after day cold rain fell from monotonous grey skies. Then we broke up for Christmas and the Kingsleys went away for a month. Sheba no longer haunted our garden and I wondered whether she had gone with them or had been sent to a boarding kennels. I reflected that if Harriet and I had not quarrelled Sheba would have been invited to stay at Springfield Farm.

The Christmas holidays seemed less exciting than usual, but I refused to admit even to myself that this was because I was missing Harriet.

Of course, I had Ian and Rodney, but they are not interested in the same things as I am. They each have a bike and they are interested in machines. They love the tractors more than they love the cows, but they spend much of their time at Lynwell Station taking the numbers of trains, which seemed to me a futile and boring occupation.

There was a meet in our village and I attended on foot and helped to hand round drinks and sandwiches. Afterwards I followed on foot—for Peppermint was too old to hunt. It poured and poured with rain, and when at last, hounds got a fox away nobody heard them go. It was altogether an unsuccessful day for everyone out, and I returned home soaking wet with chattering teeth.

I had lots of nice presents for Christmas. Mummy gave me a new riding jacket, Daddy gave me a new fountain pen and my brothers joined together to give

me a pony book which I particularly wanted. My aunts
sent money and Mrs. Biggs gave me two handkerchiefs
and I also had a few little things like penknives, scarves
and ties from Father Christmas and various friends.
I gave Mummy a pair of yellow gloves, Daddy a new
pipe, my brothers each a book, my aunts handkerchiefs
and Mrs. Biggs a pink needle-case which she loved
and I thought awful. I could not prevent myself remembering that in September I had promised to give
Harriet a copy of *In Wind And Rain,* which she wanted but could not afford, for Christmas.

I was glad the Kingsleys were away so that I need
not see Harriet on Christmas Day nor hear the sound
of their revelry.

We all went to the Boxing Day meet and followed
a little in the car, being careful not to head the fox
or foil the scent with the smell of our petrol.

Susan was out on her cob, Nutmeg, and she asked
me to come to tea one day and ride him. Bobs's
brother, Jon, was out, too, on a little bay gelding he
had hired from the Lynwell Riding Academy, and a
girl I know vaguely in the form below ours at school
dashed around without much control on a Dartmoor
pony with a little white star. I wished Peppermint was
younger and with a sound wind, and I wished my
father had thought of hiring a pony for me to hunt.
Next year, I thought, I shall ask for a hunter as my
Christmas present.

The weather turned cold after New Year's Day and
I noticed to my horror that Peppermint was growing
thinner. The vertebrae of his backbone showed
through his thick winter coat and his ribs showed. I
gave him more hay and larger feeds, but with no
visible effect. As term started he developed a cough
and I kept him in his stable during the day as well as
the night, and damped his food more lavishly than

usual. But to my horror he had begun to eat less each day. Daddy bought a tin of electuary and I put a lump the size of a walnut on his tongue three times a day.

February came in with fierce rainstorms and icy winds. It seemed to me that Peppermint was ageing each week, yet we still hesitated to call in the vet. We were secretly afraid he would advice us to have Peppermint painlessly destroyed.

"If only we can get him through the winter he'll pick up when the spring comes and he can get a bit of grass in him," said Daddy, hopefully.

But he didn't show any signs of improvement and, at last, we rang up the vet with heavy hearts. The vet is a brisk dapper little man, well known in the district for his skill in correct diagnosis. He gave Peppermint one glance and asked his age, and when Daddy said, "Over twenty," he dropped a sigh and looked at Peppermint's teeth and pulled out a wad of grass which was wedged up the side of his gums.

"This is where the trouble lies," he said. "We'll try rasping them, but I have a feeling they'll be too loose."

My heart sank. "You don't go in for red worm on your pasture, do you?" he asked as he went to the car to fetch the rasp.

"Not that I know of, but I would like to have him checked for that, anyway," said Daddy.

Pepperment's teeth *were* loose and the vet gave a groan of despair. "You said he wasn't eating well, didn't you? Well, there's the trouble all right."

"Is there nothing we can do?" I asked in a small voice.

"Well, we can't rasp them and we can't pull them out and give him a nice plastic set. He might pull through and pick up on the spring grass if you chopped up all his hay and fed him on a good deal of soft stuff, like linseed, bran and flaked maize with crushed oats, until then. And he might not. He's very thin now and his heart isn't too good," said the vet.

"We will certainly have a shot at pulling him through," said Daddy firmly.

"Right you are. I'll take a sample to test for worms all the same and drop you in a tonic to mix with his feeds to-morrow and something else for his cough," said the vet.

We went indoors after the vet had gone and had a cup of tea and discussed how to feed Peppermint. We decided he must be given lots of little feeds, and Mummy said she would feed him four times on school-days and I could give him one feed at six o'clock and one just before I went to bed. At the week-ends I would look after him entirely.

I went to bed feeling sick at heart: the next day I rose early to look at Peppermint. I pulled a polo-collared jersey and a pair of dungarees over my pyjamas and put on wellington boots and, as it was raining, Daddy's old mackintosh which hangs in the hall.

I had a strange feeling of apprehension as I crossed the stable-yard. I opened the loose-box door quietly, aware of an ominous silence and the stillness of a winter dawn.

Peppermint was lying down on his side and I noticed at once that something was wrong. Fortunately we have electric light in the cow-sheds and in the stable, and I could see clearly. Peppermint's white coat was grey with sweat and his eyes were wide open. I knelt quickly by his head and spoke softly to him, and he looked at me with a soft appealing gaze which smote my heart, I plunged my hands into my dungarees pockets and pulled out a few pieces of cow-cake, but

I knelt quickly by his head

he refused this offering. Then I felt despairing and, rushing indoors, I wakened my parents.

It took a few minutes for my words to sink in to their sleep-fuddled brains, and I cried, "Oh, hurry, hurry!"

Mummy was out of bed and in her dressing-gown first, and together we ran round to the stable.

When we entered Peppermint was trying in vain to rise to his feet.

"I expect it's his heart," said Mummy, watching him dolefully.

"He shouldn't struggle. Calm him down." But Peppermint after one more futile effort, lay still, breathing heavily.

Daddy arrived then, gave him one glance and went back indoors to ring the vet.

I sat on the floor, deep in straw, and stroked Peppermint's hot neck, and howled.

When the vet came he gave the expected verdict: "We could get him up now, but the same thing will happen again on another night in the same way," he finished.

My parents sent me indoors and I rushed past Rodney and Ian, who stood in the hall with glum faces, talking in undertones, to my room. The early morning light, cold and grey, was streaming in through my window. I looked at the photograph of Peppermint and was filled with sadness. Then I hid my head under my pillow because I could not bear to hear the fatal shot.

My parents allowed me to miss school that morning and gave me a letter of apology to give to my form mistress in the afternoon.

I arrived after lunch when everybody was resting and sat disconsolately in my form room. Presently the gang arrived, bursting with questions which I could not bear to answer. I could have told Harriet in the old days what had happened, but I could not tell Bobs or Susan or Muriel.

The form mistress was very nice and said, "That's quite all right, Andy. I quite understand and I'm very sorry. It's awful to lose an animal." And she stuffed the letter in her pocket.

Harriet was there and she opened her mouth as if to speak to me and then changed her mind. I could not forgive her for not asking "Which animal?" for not caring whether it was Blondie or Peppermint—both once such friends of hers.

My mother came over in the car and fetched me back from school at four o'clock, and in the evening my parents took me to see a film—an old but very good thriller, called *The Lady Vanishes*.

CHAPTER THREE

NEXT DAY I went to Susan's birthday party and found to my surprise that Pauline and Harriet had been invited. We all sat down to tea and Muriel was placed between Harriet and myself. She was very tactful, too obviously tactful, and I wondered for the first time whether she was enjoying our quarrel. After tea we played Murder and, as Detective, I correctly condemned Harriet to be hanged by the neck until dead, and Muriel gave a little snigger and whispered to me, "You must have enjoyed that." Of course, I had to question Harriet and she had to answer me, but I thought of myself as a brilliant young detective and not as Andy Fairfax.

Presently, I heard Susan asking Harriet if she would like to ride Nutmeg at the week-ends. I felt a wave of anger as Harriet replied with shining eyes, "Oh, yes, please. I would love it. I haven't ridden for ages and he looks awfully nice, so brisk and bouncing. Thanks terribly."

"That's super," said Susan. "Can you come over next Saturday at about half-past two?"

I wonder whether she will be punctual and whether she will manage Nutmeg? I mused. And then Muriel nudged me and said, "*She's* soon got another mount."

A moment later Harriet spoke. "I'm so sorry about Peppermint, Andy," she said, under her breath.

I suppose I could have made our quarrel up then, but Muriel's words were still fresh in my ears. "As if you care," I thought.

"Never mind. You've got Nutmeg to ride now," I replied haughtily.

Later when I was in bed that night I considered this retort and decided it had been a very silly and spiteful one. I resolved to meet Harriet on the bus on Monday and become friends once more. But, by an ill stroke of fate, Mrs. Kingsley took her to school that morning and she arrived late for prayers. Afterwards she appeared so cold that I could not bring myself to speak to her. During break Muriel told me that Harriet had said that I had become sour and small-minded. The words stung me and I resolved never to speak to Harriet again. I thought of all the rides and walks we had taken together with Peppermint and the help I had given her with Sheba and I felt I had been hard done by.

Bobs was sympathetic for she could see I was fed up. "Take no notice," she said, "Harriet's not worth bothering about, if she's like that. I've always thought her jolly stuck-up anyway—always reciting poetry and sticking her nose in the air."

March came in like a lamb that year with warm sparkling days and pearl-grey dawns. The sun cast pools of gold on our lawn's smooth slope of tender green. The crocuses were untroubled by wind or storm and the timid snowdrops looked happier than they had looked last year. Evensong's calf galloped and bucketed in damp fields and the birds seemed to sing without rest from dawn to dusk.

I missed Peppermint and felt dull without him at the week-ends. The rest of the Gang lived over three miles from Springfield Farm and I did not see very much of them out of school.

I helped Rodney and Ian make a coop for a new arrival of chicks, and I drove the tractor across the brown ploughed land.

Then, one day towards the end of March, Daddy announced suddenly that he had decided to give me a pony for my birthday present.

"But you must help choose him, too," he told me. "And I've heard of two likely animals. They've been ridden by a boy for the last three years and Jim Cooper says they are both an excellent buy. They've been hunted regularly, have won a few prizes in local gymkhanas and are both as hard as nails. I think you'll probably like one of them."

Jim Cooper is the vet and his advice is always reliable where ponies are concerned. I became very excited, though I was sure I would never find another pony as nice as Peppermint.

"Well, what do you say?" asked Daddy. "Do you want to have a look at them?"

I found my voice. "Oh, I should love to! What a wizard present! When can we go, on Saturday?"

"Well, I'll ring up and see if they will have us then. The boy is at school and father's a very busy business man, so we'll probably have to fit in with their arrangements. I gather they are fairly wealthy people but are not asking a lot for the ponies. The boy's leaving school and going up to Oxford and, anyway, he's grown out of them, but he wants to find good homes," Daddy told me.

"If Andy is having a new pony for her birthday, can I have a new watch for mine—a really good one?" asked Rodney.

"And what about my camera?" said Ian.

"Wait and see and don't be greedy," said Daddy.

"Those who ask don't get," Mummy replied firmly. "When it's *your* thirteenth birthday we'll talk about it."

"But that's ages and ages away," wailed Ian.

"What a swizz!" complained Rodney.

"You've just had new bikes," I reminded them.

"You could have had one if you had wanted it," Rodney pointed out.

"If you children are going to quarrel, *nobody* will have any presents on any birthdays. I don't know how you boys can be horrible enough to grudge Andy her pony," said Daddy. "Now get on and eat those crusts as well as the soft bread, and be quiet."

He rang up that Sunday and made an appointment to see the ponies on the following Saturday—a whole six days to wait!

"There are two chestnuts, a mare and a gelding, called Gingersnap and Brandysnap. They look like twins though they don't exactly match in colour; the mare's a golden chestnut and the gelding—he's Brandysnap—is a red chestnut," said Daddy.

"He ought to be called Rufus then," said Ian. "Andy, if you have the gelding will you call him Rufus, please, Andy, please."

"I don't know. Rufus *is* a nice name, but then so is Brandysnap. Anyway, it's all a hypothesis. They might both buck me off," I told him, imagining in my thoughts the two prancing chestnuts with flowing manes and tails.

Saturday took a long, long time to arrive, and on Friday night I could hardly sleep at all. I had told none of the other girls at school of my prospective present. I shrank from my enemy, Harriet, knowing that I was about to have another pony.

I wakened with the first swift streak of dawn on Saturday and rushed to the window to see if the day would be fine.

The sky was a soft hopeful grey, and over the grass and the sleeping flowers in our garden there hung a long strip of damp, elusive mist. The river was clear of it here and there, but looked as silent and still as the pale skies, though the cocks were waking the whole countryside with their joyous crowing and the birds were already bursting into early song.

I felt my thoughts go out to the day with the hopefulness of the dawn's vague promise and I dressed quickly.

I could hear Daddy sharpening his razor in the bathroom, and old George Brown, already out in the fields, calling up the cows to be milked.

We were to start the twenty-mile drive to see the two ponies at ten o'clock, and I planned now to take Blondie for a long walk before breakfast so that I could think about my new pony and all the adventures I would have with him—I had secretly decided on the gelding—without fear of interruption.

I laid the breakfast, so as to help Mummy, and then I called Blondie and took the winding footpath which leads down into the valley, right to the river's side.

All was quiet here, quiet and still and happy, with the lovely smells of an early spring morning. The river flowed slowly, gurgling a little where the weeds were very thick. On the slippy breen banks the old willows sadly bowed their tattered heads, as though the storms of winter had played brutal havoc with them, and were mysteriously reflected in the dark waters.

Blondie bounded gaily ahead and startled a long-legged heron into wing. I remembered the early morning when I first met Harriet, recalled our first conversation and wondered how I had been so easily misled by her easy but insincere manner.

Then my mind turned to my new pony and I saw myself competing in gymkhanas, riding to hounds, walking with dignity past Nut Tree Cottage on a handsome chestnut gelding with a touch of red in his coat. I wondered whether he had white markings and

109

whether his mane and tail were the same chestnut or a darker or lighter hue.

I would need a new larger saddle and probably a double bridle or perhaps a pelham. I knew very little about bitting, though I knew drop nosebands were in fashion and I rather fancied one of those white sheepskin nosebands which I believed a number of French race-horses wore.

I hoped my pony would be quiet and sensible to groom, and reflected that chestnuts could shine like polished gold and handsomely reward one's efforts and elbow grease. Peppermint had been often impatient and he had been a great fidget, but you could crawl between his forelegs and right underneath him when you washed his tummy and you knew he would never, never kick.

I had wandered far by this time and a feeling of emptiness reminded me that I must hurry or be late for breakfast. Calling a disappointed Blondie, I turned for home and, reaching the crest of a hill, came face to face with Harriet, who was walking Sheba. It was too late to avoid her and I almost said "Hallo," and then I remembered I was sour and small-minded and all the horrid things she had said about me to Muriel behind my back, and I tried to look haughty. She tilted her annoyingly short nose upward and with a superb look of disdain stepped aside to let me pass.

But our dogs let us down; they greeted each other with wild enthusiasm; they licked each other's noses and rushed off in a mad and happy game. I thought, let them play awhile. Why should the dogs suffer, because we are enemies?

But Harriet started to call, "Sheba, Sheba! Come here, Sheba," and the far wooded slopes echoed her words and mocked her voice and made them seem ridiculous.

110

Sheba paused for a moment with one paw in the air, and looked at Harriet with a disappointed air, then she turned and went on with the game. I should have called Blondie, but I suddenly took a wicked delight in seeing Sheba disobey Harriet.

I laughed and called out scornfully, "She's lost her manners."

Harriet blushed scarlet right up to the roots of her fair hair, and for an awful moment I thought she was going to burst into tears. Then she said, "Personally, I think you've lost yours."

"Copycat!" I called.

"Oh, you're just childish. Do try to be your age," she replied with her old coolness, pale and dignified once more.

I felt the cut of her words; she could always be so much more scathing than I.

"Sheba!" I mocked, exaggerating her tone of voice. "Sheeba, Sheeeeeba!"

Looking back, my behaviour seems stupid and babyish, but I was far too angry to care then.

"Fancy having a dog which won't come when she's called," I jeered.

"Why don't you call Blondie instead of being such a beastly little fool?" asked Harriet, and two large tears rolled down her cheeks.

Suddenly I felt all this insulting was futile and idiotic. I turned my back on her and went down over the crest calling Blondie. She *is* very good and she came at a gallop, her long red tongue hanging out and her eyes shinning with excitement. I felt I had triumphed over Harriet, but somehow the victory seemed a flat one.

I looked across to Springfield Farm, which lay snug and picturesque against its background of trees. I looked at the square smooth paddock, shaded by elms and two tall Lombardy poplars, and I thought, "Soon a chestnut pony will be grazing there, nipping the tender spring grass." The sun was rising slowly, a great fiery ball of gold and red, beyond our thin line of firs on the left of the river. The grey eastern sky was alight and glowing with colour. Turning, I saw the willows tipped with gold and the dark waters of the river glistening silver in the sunlight. The heron was strutting happily by a clump of reeds and Harriet was growing smaller and smaller as she took the winding track to Lynwell.

Suddenly I felt crestfallen. It seemed awful to be guilty of such hard words when a fine day was breaking over a warm spring countryside and all the animals were welcoming it and the hillside basked in sunlight.

CHAPTER FOUR

WE STARTED punctually and Daddy- drove us swiftly to Brook End House, which was one of those houses of character which sprang up so quickly to house stockbrokers and numerous business men in the years between the wars. Its sham beams had darkened with the years and creepers hid the newness of the bricks.

A golden labrador welcomed us as we parked the car, and Mr. Hartley, hearing the barks, came out into the drive. He was a short dark man with a noticeably large chin and small brown eyes, and he wore a well-pressed country suit and buff waistcoat.

We all shook hands politely and he said, "Well, my man has caught the pair of them up. Come round to the stables, will you?"

Two portable loose-boxes decorated the west corner of the garden and over two green doors looked two chestnut heads, both ornamented with a neat white star.

"They certainly match well," said Daddy.

"They're a bit rough now. It's the first winter they haven't been clipped, but Philip felt he had grown too heavy to ride them. The trouble is he's growing up, always thinking about dances and parties. Yet when I

The gardener led out Brandysnap first

suggested selling them he kicks up a fuss. That's why I want to get rid of them before he breaks up," Mr. Hartley explained. "But one of them is booked now, I'm afraid. I've given a friend of mine first choice. Didn't know he wanted one till he rang me up last night. He's bringing his daughter over this afternoon. She's a plucky little kid and I should like her to have one. But I didn't think it worth ringing you up because in my opinion there's nothing much to choose between

113

the two ponies. Philip never had a favourite, anyway."

I patted Gingersnap's soft, round-coated neck.

"I see," said Daddy. "Andy, you had better decide which one you want, and then if it's the same one as the other girl wants that's just too bad."

"We've another three weeks before the holidays start," Mummy added.

The gardener led out Brandysnap first and I noticed his deep girth and short hard cannon bones. He had a handsome head with large intelligent eyes and a slightly Roman nose, and his neck was long with quite a crest on it.

"Have they won anything showing?" asked Mummy.

"Yes, they've picked up a good few rosettes, though I wouldn't say they were up to Richmond standard. My son says they haven't enough blood, but they look well-bred enough to me."

"We are not looking for a little blood horse," said Daddy. "These two look just the type we want."

I mounted Brandysnap and the gardener held the bridle and the right-hand stirrup. I used my legs and turned him in the direction of the paddock Mr. Hartley pointed out to me. He was nappy and obviously did not want to leave Gingersnap.

"Those two are terribly attached to each other. They are really comic sometimes. I rather wish they could have been found a home together," said Mr. Hartley.

"You never advertised them, did you?" Mummy asked.

"No, I didn't want a lot of dealers around. Philip would never forgive me if they were sold to one of them."

Brandysnap still argued and in the end, having no stick, I hit him with the end of the reins. He bounded forward then and we reached the paddock gate in a few strides. I felt very high up and his neck seemed very long after Peppermint's little short one.

He didn't want to open the gate, but after a short argument I managed to make him stand still while I undid the latch.

"Of course neither of these ponies has been ridden for a good many months, so they are bound to be a little out of hand," said Mr. Hartley.

Brandysnap was still thinking of Gingersnap, as I rode round the paddock and when she neighed he answered. He had nice even paces, good head carriage, and a long walk when he was going towards Gingersnap. He was inclined to put down his head when I tried to slow him up, but I supposed I should drive his hocks under him and I wasn't using my legs enough. He did not seem to back very straight, but he jumped the pair of hurdles, which the gardener had erected, beautifully, and he jumped so high that he nearly jumped me off. I lost both stirrups, clung round his neck and then regained my seat.

"Well done! Bravo! Well set!" called Mr. Hartley, and I wondered why so many people congratulate you when you have nearly fallen off.

While I had been clinging round Brandysnap's neck he had taken me to the gate, and he now neighed again to Gingersnap and I had a little tussle to make him go round the paddock another time.

Next time I jumped I remained secure, and then Daddy said, "What about trying the other one now, Andy?"

Mr. Hartley called, "Bert! Bring the mare round, please."

I dismounted and a moment later the gardener arrived with Gingersnap, who, like Brandysnap, wore a pelham with a scarlet brow band.

She seemed easier to ride and jumped with more

115

scope, but her head carriage was not quite so good and she poked her nose a little. She neighed to the retreating Brandysnap and tried to sidle towards the gate.

I rode her hard but her thoughts seemed elsewhere, down in the loose-box with her friend, and I could not get her entire attention. She had a beautiful trot, when she was going towards the stable, very cadenced and full of impulsion.

After a while Mummy called out, "I think you've tried her enough now. Come and tell us which you like best."

I thought carefully as I rode across the paddock. Gingersnap had the better paces, but I had fallen in love with Brandysnap's colour and before I left home I had decided on the gelding.

My parents looked cold and I realised that I must have been riding for nearly an hour. Mr. Hartley looked impatient and was stamping his feet and banging his hands together. The sun was hidden now by thick white clouds, which had come up from the east, and a bitter wind was blowing.

"Come on, Andy. We're half frozen," said Daddy.

"Made up your mind?" asked Mummy again.

I thought of Brandysnap's head looking over the loosebox door at home, the white star set in the red chestnut of his coat; and I forgot Gingersnap's cadence and scope.

"Brandysnap," I said firmly.

"Right," said Daddy." Mr. Hartley and I have discussed the price and we are both quite satisfied, so if his friend's daughter doesn't take a fancy to the same pony you can have him."

"Oh, thank you!" I said. "Thank you."

"And supposing the girl wants the gelding, will you have Gingersnap?" asked Daddy.

"Oh, I don't know," I answered, as I dismounted and patted her golden neck. "I don't like her nearly as much as Brandysnap, though I know she's lovely."

"I think she's got a better front, actually," said Daddy, "and a much better jump, but it's your birthday. The important thing is that *you* should like the pony."

"Yes, I definitely like Brandysnap best," I told them decisively.

We talked about the two ponies all the way home. "Oh, I *do* hope she doesn't choose him. It will be dreadful if she does," I said.

Then Daddy suddenly began to remember all the things we had forgotten to do.

"We forgot to try them on the road," he said forlornly. "They may be awful in traffic and we never even watched them saddled; they may kick like anything when the girths are tightened."

"Oh, stop worrying, Guy!" said Mummy. "Cooper said they were a good sound couple of ponies. He's Hartley's vet as well as ours and an honest man. It wouldn't be worth his while to recommend unsound or dangerous ponies. Besides, he's known Andy for years and wouldn't dream of suggesting anything unreliable. If Andy broke her neck he would never forgive himself."

"I shall get at least two hunts before the end of the season," I reflected.

"Yes, but remember those ponies aren't fit. You couldn't keep them out a whole day," Daddy reminded me.

We stopped at a small hotel for lunch on the way home and I gave Blondie, who had been kept in the car while we tried the ponies, a run on a cold windy village green.

The weather had certainly changed for the worse

117

and all the sparkle of spring had left the darkening landscape. Great black clouds rolled up from the east like billows of factory smoke. The trees trembled and creaked as though afraid and the young grass trembled. A few balls of icy hail hit the car's windscreen.

"I pity the child who tries the ponies this afternoon," said Mummy.

"She *must* choose Gingersnap, she *must*! I shall will her," I declared, and then I started to mutter, "Fall off Brandysnap. Choose Gingersnap," over and over again.

"If the girl falls off and hurts herself you'll be haunted by remorse," said Mummy.

"It's no good willing yet. She won't even be there," added Daddy.

The afternoon passed very, very slowly and I couldn't settle down. I helped feed some young calves. I milked Evensong and I took Blondie for a walk. I reflected that if Harriet had been here we could have talked the whole thing over together, planned the first ride. She would have been nearly as excited as myself and I hated her now for having deserted me. I discussed it with Blondie, but, although she is generally a good listener, to-day she was more interested in rabbit hunting. Rodney and Ian took a polite interest and tried to persuade me to change Brandysnap's name to Rufus.

I wished they had taken to riding instead of bicycles, but in spite of all this I was wildly excited. Every now and then I asked Mummy to telephone Mr. Hartley to ask which pony had been chosen by the girl, until she became exasperated and told me to go away and read a book or do my prep. Of course, prep. was impossible; my mind would not and could not concentrate on French verbs or Latin declensions.

118

At last is was five o'clock and Mummy said, "You can go and ring up now, Andy," and Daddy said, "Call me if it's Brandysnap, then I'll make the arrangements about boxing and everything."

Mr. Hartley answered the telephone and for a moment I was so excited I could not collect my wits.

"Oh, this is Andy," I said at last. (She must have chosen Gingersnap, she *must*, said my thoughts.)

"I've got bad news for you, I'm afraid," Mr. Hartley's suave voice told me. I felt a wave of disappointment. Why had I not realised the girl was *certain* to fall for Brandysnap? Why did I ever allow myself to hope she wouldn't? At that moment I wanted Brandysnap more than any other pony in the whole wide world and I couldn't speak because of the lump rising in my throat.

"Did you hear? I'm sorry, Andy. Why don't you have the mare instead; she's every bit as good?" asked Mr. Hartley.

My voice said, "Thank you. Yes, I heard. Daddy wants to speak to you. Hold on, please."

"It's no good. She chose Brandysnap. I should have known she would—and I did want him so!" I told my parents.

"Never mind," said Mummy. "We'll find another. And, for goodness' sake, don't talk in that whine."

"There's no point in my speaking. If you don't want the mare instead there's nothing to arrange, so that's that," said Daddy.

"Why don't you have Gingersnap? I thought she was the nicer of the two, though I didn't like to say so because the pony is your present, after all," asked Mummy.

"I wanted *Brandysnap*," I said obstinately.

Daddy picked up the receiver. "I'm sorry to hear you've sold the gelding. Andy had set her heart on

119

him," he said, and then, after a pause when he must have been listening to Mr. Hartley, "No, she doesn't like the mare. Yes, well, look here: if she changes her mind about that I'll give you a ring later to-night. I agree with you. I liked the mare best from the start. She's got more quality and she moves well, but Andy fell in love with Brandysnap at sight and now she's disappointed. Yes, right you are; let's leave it like that. Good-bye."

"That's a pity," he said, putting down the receiver.

"We must start looking round for something else, though I don't think we will do better than Gingersnap, not for the price, anyway. Ponies, with gymkhana and hunting experience, of round about fourteen hands are difficult to find, but still we've got another three weeks before your birthday, haven't we?"

"I shall miss the two hunts now," I said.

"Are you *quite* sure you couldn't get to like Gingersnap?" asked Mummy. "After all, a mare has some advantages. When she is getting on you can breed from her."

"That's true," I said slowly, trying to banish the picture of a red-chestnut neck, a slightly roman nose and a dazzling star from my mind.

"She looked a comfier ride," added Mummy.

"I don't know, I just don't know. I want to think about it," I said.

Rodney and Ian came dashing into the room then. "Have you got him? When's he coming? Will you call him Rufus? Will you hunt on Saturday?" they asked together.

"But why? What's happened?" I heard Ian say, as I wandered up to the nursery.

I tried to do my prep. again, but now my mind wandered to Gingersnap. She had a nice head, too—really a better head than Brandysnap's, with more breeding. I don't know why I had been attracted by a roman nose. I remembered that Gingersnap had not been quite so nappy and would look better when her summer coat came through. By supper-time I had decided to have her.

My parents were both pleased. They had always liked her the best of the two.

"As soon as you've eaten that welsh rarebit, ring up Mr. Hartley and tell him, and say I'll send Stevens round with his cattle truck after he's taken the bull calves down on Monday—that will be about twelve o'clock—and I'll put the cheque in the post to-night," said Daddy.

Mr. Hartley sounded very pleased, but that, I suppose, was to be expected.

"I think you are very wise and she's a nice pony for a girl, very quiet to groom and gentle," he said

"It will be nice having a mare, because if she falls down on the road or anything awful I could breed from her, couldn't I?" I suggested, more to convince myself than Mr. Hartley.

"I'm sure you will never regret having her," he told me with conviction. "By the way, do you know the little girl who chose to have Brandysnap lives near you? . . . Nut Tree Cottage. John Kingsley is a good friend of mine, and she's a plucky little kid."

"Of course," I said faintly. "Harriet."

"That's right, Harriet. It will be nice having two ponies in the same village. It seems silly really that we didn't think to send them in the same box. I am sure if you rang the Kingsleys they would be only too pleased to let Ginger travel over with Brandy. . . ."

He seemed in a conversational mood and he talked on about this and that; and I longed for him to stop, so that I could sit down and think for a moment.

He paused at last and I said, "Daddy's arranged

about the box already, I'm afraid," and then I told him the arrangements and thanked him, and rang off.

So Harriet had Brandysnap! The portable loose-box would be erected and he would live opposite. Of course *she* would choose him. His colour, his name and his proud carriage would win *her* every time. I started to convince myself very hard that Gingersnap was the better of the two ponies, that I had really liked her best from the first. I did not want Harriet to know that I had chosen Brandysnap first; she must never know that. I told myself that I had a better eye for a horse than Harriet. I was not to be swayed by colour. Gingersnap was better put together; she had more quality and not so much knee action at the trot. I sat in one of my parents' deep comfy arm-chairs and presently Blondie appeared and, jumping on my knee, covered my face with kisses.

Then Daddy and Mummy came into the room and said, "All arranged?"

"Yes, thank you. He was awfully pleased," I said.

"Are *you* pleased? That's the point. You don't look on top of the world," observed Mummy. "You're not still hankering after Brandsnap, are you?"

I couldn't bring myself to tell them about Harriet just then.

"I was only thinking," I said defensively. "Of course I'm pleased. Thank you both terribly. I think I will go to bed now. Will you come up and say good night?"

As I left the room and climbed the steep back stairs to bed, I heard Mummy say, "I expect she's tired. It's all the excitement. She'll be better after a good night's sleep," and I wished I didn't feel so flat, for really I was longing for Gingersnap to arrive.

CHAPTER FIVE

WHEN I came back from school on Monday, Gingersnap was looking over my loose-box door at home, gazing with distracted eyes towards Nut Tree Cottage. She gave a loud, frantic neigh as I approached, and I heard Brandysnap answer from across the road. I gave her a couple of carrots and she gobbled them and then let out another deafening neigh and rushed round the box.

Daddy appeared from the cow-sheds. "I should put her out in the paddock now. I only kept her in for you to see and she's used to living out. What's the horse answering her?"

"He's Brandysnap. Harriet is the friend's daughter and she chose him. Mr. Hartley told me on Saturday night," I said, and then I hurried away to find a halter.

Daddy had gone when I returned and Gingersnap seemed demented. She dashed round the box and neighed and neighed; and I could hear Brandysnap galloping round the Kingsleys' paddock, and answering in a shrill and hysterical way. It was some moments before I could make Gingersnap stand still to have the halter put on and, when I eventually led her out, she trod on my toes in her excitement.

Once out in our paddock, she could see Brandysnap, and they both gave glad neighs of recognition. Harriet saw me but I could not see the expression on her face. I wondered, not for the first time, whether Mr. Hartley told her that I was the child who came in the morning and whether she knew I had wanted Brandysnap. Dusk was falling, and Gingersnap looked very striking as she stood, silhouetted against the darkening sky, with flowing mane and tail, erect head and large liquid eyes gazing across the road to Brandy-snap. I admired the length of her neck and shoulders and the delicate cut of her ears. Then suddenly she wheeled and with a wild neigh started to gallop round the paddock.

She certainly moved well and for a moment I could not take my eyes off her. Then I suddenly remembered I had not thanked my parents properly for her; I had been most dismal to Daddy in the yard and I recalled with horror how unenthusiastic I had been on Saturday evening.

I simply shot indoors and fell over Ian, who let out a loud roar. "Sorry, dreadfully sorry," I muttered. "Are you all right?"

"My leg! Oh, my leg!" wailed Ian.

I helped him up and looked at his leg; there was nothing wrong to see. "Never mind," I said. "It'll soon be all right. Have you seen Gingersnap?"

He hadn't and in the excitement of hearing she was in the paddock he forgot his leg.

I was telling my parents how beautifully she moved, when I heard Rodney and Ian shrieking at the top of their voices. The noise came from the direction of the paddock and I dashed there as fast as my legs would carry me.

"She's gone!" yelled Ian.

"She jumped right in front of our very eyes!" yelled Rodney.

"Where, where?" I called, racing across the lawn.

"Out into the road and now we can't see her! It's too dark!" they both shrieked together.

"Gosh, it was a super jump!" added Rodney.

"She'll be with Brandysnap now," I said, slowing down to a walk and realising the neighing had stopped and all was quiet in the Kingsley's paddock.

"Brandysnap, Brandysnap? What *are* you talking
124

about?" asked Rodney.

"Harriet's got him. She was the girl I told you about. But I definitely like Gingersnap best now. I'm glad I've got her now," I said shortly.

"She's a wizard jumper . . . honestly!" said Rodney.

I climbed the fence and crossed the road, and there in the Kingsleys' little paddock I could see two figures —Gingersnap and Brandysnap standing quietly side by side.

I remembered I had no halter and no tait-bit. I called softly to Rodney, asking him to fetch them for me, but he didn't hear and then I shouted, and that started Sheba barking in Nut Tree Cottage.

"Come along, come along—coop, coop," I said quietly, approaching the two ponies. They threw up their heads, gave me one startled glance and then, with a couple of snorts, galloped away across the dew-wet grass. I remembered suddenly that we had never asked Mr. Hartley if they were good to be caught. I might spend all night following Gingersnap round the field! And then not catch her. I waited until the ponies had quietened down again and Rodney had obligingly returned with the halter and three carrots.

Then, holding out a carrot and saying," Gingersnap, whoa my little Gingersnap." I tried again.

But the two ponies walked briskly away with their tails kinked high over their backs.

The moon had not come up yet and it was very dark, and the ponies did not know me.

"Please can you possibly get me a bucket of oats?" I asked my brothers

"Where are they now? We don't know." said Rodney.

"All right, never mind, I'll go," I told them.

I went round to the barn and feached some, and

then my parents appeared and said the boys had told them what had happened. Had Gingersnap hurt herself? I told them it was too dark to see, but she didn't look lame.

We had a try with the bucket of oats, but in vain. We couldn't get within twenty yards of the ponies, and they were obviously wildly excited.

"The only thing you can do," said Daddy, "is to ask the Kingsleys if you can leave Gingersnap in there for the night. You must explain what happened."

"Oh no!" I said.

"Andy doesn't want to do that, because of the ridiculous quarrel she's had with Harriet," said Mummy.

"Well, this is a good opportunity to make it up, and about time too," said Daddy. "Go on, Andy, do as you're told."

"I'll go," volunteered Rodney.

"No. It's Andy's pony and she must look after it," said Daddy firmly.

There was no way out. I crossed the little paddock and walked down the little path, which Harriet calls the Nut Walk, because there are nut trees on either side, and stepped over the paving stones to the front door. I knew the garden so well, had so often played there with Harriet in the past, that I could easily find my way in the dark. A light shone from the parlour window, through the expensive cottagey curtains, which Mrs. Kingsley had bought in London.

I hesitated, thinking what I would say when Harriet answered the door, and then I knocked and the knock seemed to ring right through the cottage. I heard the ponies snorting in the paddock and the sound of galloping hoofs on wet grass, and I realised Daddy was having another try. Then the little oak door opened to reveal Mrs. Kingsley. I was so surprised not to see Harriet that I gave a little gasp and fell silent.

"Do you want to see Harriet? She's cleaning her new tack in the kitchen," said Mrs. Kingsley.

"Oh, no," I said. And then I explained. "Do you mind terribly if we leave Gingersnap in there till morning?" I finished.

"But, of course, my dear. That's quite all right. I expect Brandysnap will be thrilled to have her there; he was terribly lonely. But we never realised you were the other customer. How thrilling!" said Mrs. Kingsley with her sparkling smile.

I thanked her and went away, sorry now that I had not seen Harriet.

"It's all right. We can leave her there," I told my parents.

"Are you friends again now?" asked Daddy.

"No fear. Not with *her*. It's a feud to the death," I said firmly.

I had some prep, to do and once again I could not concentrate, but I finished it somehow and went to sleep thinking of the low marks I would get on the morrow.

Daddy had promised to waken me early, as he expected to be up most of the night with a calving cow, so I could catch Gingersnap before going to school next morning.

It was a wet cold dawn, and Daddy said, "Leave her, Andy. George and I will have a try later on."

But, once awake, I was determined to catch Gingersnap myself. After all, she's *my* pony, I thought with pleasure. I dressed in dungarees and polo-collared pullover and, collecting the halter and oats and donning a mac, I hurried out into the rain.

Gingersnap and Brandysnap were standing together. looking very sweet, under a sycamore tree and the

127

rain had smoothed their manes and coats, giving them a sleek appearance. I rattled the bucket hopefully and they looked across at me and pricked their ears.

All the excitement of the evening before seemed to have left them and presently they came up to me, and I caught Gingersnap quite easily. I led her to the little gate, which opens into the Kingsleys' garden, and then down the Nut Walk into the road. Harriet looked out of a window, but did not wave.

The rain started to come down in torrents and Gingersnap bowed her head and then suddenly stopped, digging in her toes and uttering a loud neigh. I had a job to get her along after that and I was soaked by the time we reached the stable.

George called to me to run indoors and kindly offered to get her hay and water. Blondie came racing from the garden and covered me with wet paw-marks, and, from an upstairs window, Mummy called, "Hurry up, Andy. It's breakfast and you'll be late to school at this rate."

CHAPTER SIX

I KEPT Gingersnap in our Long Meadow with our milking cows from then on. She could not see Brandysnap and the fences were high, so she did not jump out again. I rose early three mornings that week and rode her for half an hour before breakfast. I schooled her in the Long Meadow and taught her to rein back without throwing up her head, and I trotted her in circles round a big oak tree.

I wanted her fit enough to ride to the meet at Brewers' Green on Saturday. Daddy told me the coloured brow band was in bad taste and ought to be changed for a leather one. I thought of Harriet, de-

I trotted round a big oak tree

cided our ponies mustn't match and agreed with him.

I also decided I must change Gingersnap's name.
because it too obviously matched with Brandysnap
and I knew Harriet was too superstitious to change
his. Anyway, Brandysnap was a name which would
probably appeal to her and I did not particularly like
Gingersnap.

Ian wanted me to choose Star and Rodney wanted
Goldpiece, and my parents suggested Celandine,
Goldust and Copper.

In the end I decided on Celandine, although
Mummy said she wasn't exactly the colour of one.

Saturday dawned fine and fair, with a light breeze
stirring the trees and chasing a host of frilly clouds
across spring skies.

Gingersnap was easy to catch, and by ten o'clock I
was ready to start for Brewers' Green. I hoped Harriet

E

would not be taking Brandysnap to the meet as I rode away down the drive. And I reminded myself that my pony was now called Celandine. I had not plaited her mane as I was not actually proposing to hunt, and her coat was long and my clothes old, but I guessed that Harriet would be well turned out.

However, a piercing neigh told me Brandysnap was still in the Kingsleys' paddock and, before I could think further, Celandine was on the bank trying to force her way through the hedge to join him. I hate arguing with a pony on a bank, because you never know when they are going to fall off sideways or backwards, and I tried to use the utmost tact to turn her round so we could go down again with safety.

But Celandine only had one aim in view—to be in with Brandysnap again—and she took no notice of me at all.

I was still struggling with her when Harriet came sauntering by with Sheba. She pretended to look in the other direction, but I knew she had seen me and I felt furious. I raised my stick and hit Celandine sharply behind my leg and she gave a leap of surprise which landed her on the hard rough road with a bang.

I rode by Harriet at a brisk trot and saw her turn and take a footpath across our field in the direction of Brewers' Green.

Then, a few minutes later, I heard galloping hoofbeats behind me. Celandine neighed; a piercing neigh answered her, and then Brandysnap, puffing and blowing, was at our side.

For a few seconds I didn't know what I was going to do. I pulled up and tried to collect my wits. The time was a quarter past ten; it was three miles to the meet and half a mile back to Nut Tree Cottage. But I knew I must retrace my footsteps and put Brandysnap

130

back in his paddock.

Celandine was pleased to turn for home and happy to have her old friend jogging at her side, and I realised for the first time how hard it must be for the two ponies to be parted, how lonely for each of them to live alone. If Harriet and I had not quarrelled they could have lived together. I looked at Brandysnap, his bright coat dusty now in the sun, his mane blown hither and thither by the wind, and I realised that I far preferred Celandine now.

When I reached Nut Tree Cottage, I found Brandysnap had broken down part of the hedge, leaving a big gap, and if I put him back he would most certainly walk out again.

Time was getting short and there was no sign of either of the Kingsley parents, so I rode up our drive, tempted him into one of our loose-boxes, slammed the door and shouted and asked George to let the Kingsleys know.

Celandine was reluctant to leave the yard; she neighed and argued and ran backwards, and wasted valuable minutes. In the end I lost my temper and whacked her as hard as I could and then she dashed out into the road at a brisk trot, and we were nearly run over.

I arrived at Brewers Green hot and bothered, and five minutes late. Celandine was sweating and her coat was sticky.

I heard Harriet saying in a loud voice to Susan that she had not considered Brandysnap fit enough to bring over. "After all, he hasn't been ridden for months," she said.

I didn't bother to tell her his whereabouts, because I thought it was better for George to tell the parents.

Hounds were gathered outside The Thistle and Crown, a long, low village pub with warped doors and tiny lattice windows, and, every now and then, one would slip through into the bar and be chivvied out by some loud-voiced farmer. It was a small field with only three scarlet coats—the hunt staff's and the Master's—but the merry scene, the jingle of bit and stirrup, the creaking of leather and the squelch of hoof on grass, stirred me as much as always, and I felt Celandine trembling with excitement.

Next week we shall be following, I thought, and I saw myself up in the front, close to the Master's grey mare, taking hedges and posts and rails in my stride.

"Hallo!" called Jon. "Bobs said you had a new pony, but, I say, what a smasher!"

"He's awfully like Harriet's new one," remarked Susan. "Yes, but *she*, not *he*," I said firmly.

"What's *she* called?" asked the girl from school with the Dartmoor pony—I remembered suddenly that her name was Gillian.

"Celandine," I told them, and I realized Harriet heard my words.

"Hounds, please!" said the Master, and then the huntsman rode his bay cob across the green with all the glory of black and tan, lemon and white around him, and the whipper-in, resplendent in scarlet, brought up the rear; and the horn rang out and echoed in the sunlit woods and the hills beyond the shining silver river.

It seemed hard to tear myself away from it all, but Daddy was at my side. "No, come on, no following. Your pony's not fit enough. You'll break her wind. You can have half a day next week," he said.

I remembered poor little Peppermint and turned a disappointed Celandine for home. Harriet was getting a lift back. I saw her stepping into a Fiat which belongs to a young married couple who live in our village.

Celandine was hot and excited and neighed frequently. I wondered if she neighed as much when Philip Hartley hunted her, and then I remembered she hadn't been parted from Brandysnap at all for over six months.

When I reached home I was welcomed by an hysterical whinney and I realised Brandysnap was still in one of our loose-boxes. At the same moment I saw Mr. and Mrs. Kingsley turn up the drive in their coupé and call out, "Not a sign anywhere."

At first I wondered what on earth they were talking about, and then suddenly it occurred to me that perhaps George had never told them about Brandysnap, perhaps they were searching for him.

I pushed a joyful Celandine into her box and took off her tack, and the next moment Harriet was in the yard.

"Have you by any chance seen Brandysnap, please?" she asked coldly.

"Didn't George tell you?" I said "I say, I *am* sorry. He's in this loose-box. He's been there since half-past ten."

"We've been searching the whole countryside—or rather my parents have. Next time you shut *my* pony in one of your stables could you kindly let me know," said Harriet.

I felt furious. I didn't try to explain. "Next time I'll leave him on the roads, if you like," I said, flinging the top door wide, so Brandysnap was looking out. Then I walked away to the saddle-room, ignoring Harriet's "Sorry," because I didn't want to make it up. I didn't want to be friends again, or rather I thought I didn't.

On Sunday I went out for a ride, diving deep down into the woods where little clumps of snowdrops gleamed white against the trunks, and the green leaves

133

of the bluebell plants pushed through last year's leaves.

Celandine had not wanted to start out for the ride and had called to Brandysnap, but now she seemed to have settled down and walked with long swinging strides and high head carriage as though filled with the joy of spring. My thoughts were far away when suddenly I felt her stride shorten and saw her nostrils quiver, as though she was suddenly on the alert. Then she neighed, a long loud neigh which reached the wide outskirts of the woods and came back a mocking echo, and I heard the squelch of hoofs on damp earth and the clink of a bit. Someone was coming round the bend at a brisk trot and, in a moment, I saw that someone was Harriet on Brandysnap. She was out of control and she had lost her stirrups, for Brandysnap had heard Celandine's anguished neigh and had taken charge. The two ponies whinnied to each other in glad recognition, came to an abrupt halt and sniffed noses.

"Brandysnap!" exclaimed Harriet, trying to turn him away.

"Come on, Gingersnap! Walk on!" I said, forgetting her new name. But we both spoke in vain. The ponies argued and my stirrup banged Harriet's ankle.

"Oh, don't! Do move out of the way," she said peevishly.

"If *you* would move, I *might* be able to," I replied angrily.

Still the ponies clung close together. I raised my hand to hit Celandine, but at the same moment Brandysnap bumped against my leg and, instead of the stick hitting Celandine, it landed with a loud whack on Harriet's leg.

"Oh, you beast!" she said. And she raised her hand as though to hit me, but, leaning down, I dodged, and

134

managed to turn Celandine in the direction of home. I did not mind which way I went as long as I was rid of Harriet, but Brandysnap had other ideas and he came too, ignoring his rider's vigorous efforts. Neither Harriet nor I had had much tuition in riding during our lives and I believed we were both at a loss; and the worst of it was, we were both in bad tempers and could not think coolly.

"*Will* you go away?" stormed Harriet.

"I am going away, only you insist on coming with me," I retorted furiously.

"You are not. You are going in the opposite direction to the one you were going when I met you," contradicted Harriet.

This was true, I realised. "All right," I said. "I'll go the other way then. I couldn't care less."

I started to turn Celandine, but she bucked and I lost my stirrups, and then she dashed forward with Brandysnap, so Harriet's foot hit my ankle, and I yelled "Ow!"

I whacked Celandine then as hard as I could, and she broke into a canter, and Brandysnap cantered beside her. We rode down the track like a couple of old friends, but we were both struggling to pull up.

At last I stopped Celandine. "Look," I said angrily. "I'm going to dismount and hold Gingersnap and you can ride on. I'll give you five minutes' start and then I'm going to ride back the way I came, otherwise I shall be late for lunch."

It was the longest sentence I had spoken to Harriet for months.

"Okay, thanks," she said.

I jumped to the ground and held Celandine's two reins behind the bit. "Ride on," I said.

She disappeared round the corner, with many a backward glance from Brandysnap. Celandine neighed, and neighed again, and then she trod on my big toe, and tugged so hard at the reins that I thought she would pull my arm out of its socket.

I looked at my watch and the time was a quarter to one. In another two minutes I shall mount, I thought, and I turned to watch a squirrel run up a tree. That moment was my undoing. Celandine gave another tug and, in the act of turning, I had all my weight on one foot, so she over-balanced me and I fell face forward into the soft brown earth and bit a mouthful of good wet mud. The reins slipped from my hands and, with a thud of hoofs, and a ringing neigh, Celandine disappeared from sight in pursuit of her darling Brandysnap.

I picked up myself slowly and spat out some mud, and inwardly cursed myself for a fool. Then I started to walk for home. I had no hope that Celandine might stop at the wayside to eat grass; she would gallop on until she caught up with her friend and Harriet.

And what will Harriet do? I asked myself and I knew in my heart of hearts that she would do the right thing; she would catch Celandine and ride back to find me; and I would have to thank her nicely, though she was my enemy and a false friend.

Presently I heard the sound of hoofs again and Harriet's voice called. "Got her! I've caught her. Are you all right?"

And I felt so annoyed I could only answer sulkily.

"Buck up, then." Looking back, it surprises me that neither of us saw the funny side, because it *was* funny and I must have been an odd sight with my face coated with mud.

But I said, "Thank you" with bad grace, and mounted hastily, without looking Harriet in the face.

"It's so late that I think perhaps we had better ride back together. We needn't speak," said Harriet.

"All right. Buck up. Let's trot," I retorted shortly.

The ponies were in high spirits now and they started for home with a great flourish, fully aware of their triumph.

We were both excessively polite and at the gateway from the wood we both stood back so the other one might go first, until, in exasperation, Celandine dashed forward, banging my legs on the posts, in an effort to settle the matter.

We met George as we rode down the narrow uphill road which leads to Nut Tree Cottage and Springfield Farm, and he looked at us with surprise and pleasure, as though he was pleased to see us together.

The ponies argued when we had to leave each other at our respective gates and I think we were both near losing our tempers.

I was late for lunch, but my parents were not angry; they positively beamed, which seemed strange, because normally they don't like it if I'm late on Sundays, though they are exceptionally decent about the other days of the week.

At last Ian said, "Do you like Harriet again now, Andy?"

And Mummy hastily added, "I'm glad you've both stopped being so silly. It will be nicer for you to have someone to ride with again."

I looked from one to the other and they both seemed truly pleased. "I'm sorry," I said. "But we are still deadly enemies."

"But I saw you riding through the village like old friends," said Mummy with surprise. "What on earth are you two up to now?"

"That, was just coincidence. We didn't speak to one another," I explained. I couldn't bring myself to tell them I could not control Celandine.

"I think you are both behaving very stupidly, and

137

it's about time you snapped out of it," said Daddy. "Here you are, both the same age, with the same interests, living opposite each other with two boxer dogs and two chestnut ponies, and you won't speak to each other because of some trivial incident which occurred ages ago. Do be your age!"

"You don't understand and you don't know the details. Honestly, it wasn't trivial and, anyway, we find we haven't much in common; we find each other small-minded. Surely we can change our minds. I never want to speak to Harriet again. She's a false friend, she's twofaced. You should hear the things she's told Muriel about me, *then* you wouldn't want us to be friends again," I ended vehemently.

"You are both being silly and idiotic and, as for Muriel, I wouldn't trust her an inch. You've only got to look at her face to see she's a trouble-maker," said Daddy; and then he got up to carve second helpings of chicken and that was the end of the conversation.

CHAPTER SEVEN

WE BROKE up on the next Wednesday, and Thursday was the date of the Children's Meet, so I hardly listened to all the farewells, because my mind was full of thoughts of the following day.

It was early April and fair weather was with us, bringing forward the young grass, the seeds and the first tender leaves. Once again I rose to find a pearly dawn, swift and silent and fine as gossamer. Softly the sleeping countryside wakened to another day and the wooded slopes lay dark against the lightening sky beyond a shrouded river and the sad weeping willows and the distant crowing of our stock cockerels. Here was no long and dismal dawn when morale is low, but another dawn full of hope and indescribable gladness; and fragile shades of grey, and elusiveness.

Filled with energy, I rushed to the stable and fed and watered Celandine, but she was not interested in her food; she was calling to Brandysnap, who was answering and kicking his stable door.

The Kingsleys' portable loose-box was up at last and I suppose Harriet had kept him in through the night, so he could not escape and join Celandine. I had kept *her* in so she could not join Brandysnap.

Her neighing irritated me a little; it was so deafening, and I wanted her to eat. Every time Brandysnap answered she took a quick turn round her box, churning up the long golden straw, before giving her frantic call. As she obviously had no intention of eating her feed, I tied her up to a ring in the wall and set to work with a dandy brush. It was difficult to groom her well, because she would not stand still; but her coat had started to come out and underneath was a new and glossy summer coat. I had to stop every now and then to clean the curry comb and, all too soon, I heard Mummy called, "Breakfast!" I left Celandine to eat her feed and hurried indoors.

I had just eaten my porridge when Mummy looked out of the window and said, "There's your pony in the garden, galloping across the lawn and cutting up the turf—Daddy will be furious."

I rushed out and nearly ran into Harriet, who was hurrying past our front door in the wake of Brandysnap. "He knocked me down when I went in with his feed," she panted.

"Chasing won't do any good." I said, and then I remembered we were enemies and not on speaking terms. I noticed Sheba and Blondie playing joyfully

139

on the lawn, before I slowly followed Harriet.

Celandine and Brandysnap were having a touching reunion when I reached the stable-yard, and Harriet was trying vainly to push their noses apart so that she could put a halter on Brandysnap.

"It's all Gingersnap's fault—neigh, neigh, neigh, all day long. Of course Brandysnap gets upset," she said angrily.

"Her name is *not* Gingersnap. It has been changed to Celandine, and . . ."

"That will bring you bad luck," said the ever superstitious Harriet.

"And," I continued, with dignity, "what about Brandysnap—doesn't he ever neigh?"

"Gingersnap starts it; you know jolly well she does," said Harriet, getting the halter on at last.

"What nonsense!" I explained. "Brandysnap is at *least* as bad. And, if you must talk, please call Celandine by her proper name."

"Oh, I'm off. You bore me stiff with your pettiness," said Harriet, tugging at Brandysnap.

The words stung me and, to my fury, I felt tears smarting in my eyes. I turned away and waited to hear the sound of retreating hoofs, but only the sound of scraping hoofs on gravel reached my ears. I looked round and saw that Brandysnap had dug his toes in; Harriet was trying in vain to drag him down the drive, and she was growing very red in the face.

I began to laugh suddenly—not at Harriet, but at both of us and our ponies. I looked at Celandine, who was watching Brandysnap with an anxious expression on her face, and then I saw our two dogs playing in the garden and giggled again.

Harriet thought I was laughing scornfully at her own unsuccessful efforts, and she was near tears.

"I shall never get to the meet in time now," she said.

Harriet was trying in vain to drag him down the drive

"If you weren't an absolute beast you would hit him on the quarters. But, of course, you always did have a spiteful sense of humour."

I knew her last sentence wasn't true and I was calm enough now to know she did not believe it herself. I picked up a halter and gave Brandysnap a sharp rap; and he leapt forward, and rushed down the drive. Celandine neighed and he stopped again, so I ran down and hit him once more; and then he was out on the road and well on the way to his loose-box.

Harriet called back a reluctant "Thank you," and I returned to breakfast, feeling oddly light-hearted.

Soon Mummy was tying my hunting tie and giving me advice, for she had hunted herself when she was a child.

"Take your turn at any jumps and don't push, and if you refuse get out of the way and let someone else

141

have a try. Remember, don't press hounds and don't ride on horses' tails. If you see a horse with a red ribbon keep right away. . . . I don't want you coming back with a broken leg. If you see a fox break cover don't holler if hounds are on a line and, anyway, count ten slowly before you holler. You mustn't frighten him back into covert. . . ."

There seemed a lot to remember and I wondered how much I would forget when I was really excited. And then I wondered how much Harriet knew about hunting etiquette and manners.

"If someone dismounts to open a gate for you, don't gallop away and leave him, but wait until he has mounted again. Open all the gates you can for other people. Don't sit gaping and expect your elders to do it for you. . . ." Mummy continued, as she stuck in my large gold stock pin.

Presently, I was in the stable-yard and then I was riding out on the road, and the sun was breaking through the thin veil of clouds and lying in pale shafts across the tarmac. The birds were singing with all the ardour of spring, and the air was light and fresh with the smell of earth and grass and flowers.

I cracked my new hunting whip and Celandine sprang forward into a canter. I brought her back into a walk, but she would not settle, and soon I realised that Harriet and Brandysnap were just ahead and I was gaining on them. Presently Celandine neighed and, of course, Brandysnap answered, and from that moment my four-mile hack to the meet was spoilt. She jogged the whole way and at every opportunity she broke into a canter.

I wondered how Harriet was faring. Was Brandysnap stopping every now and then to look reluctantly back in the hope of seeing his friend? Was she finding it difficult to make him go at all? Was he being dreadfully nappy?

Once or twice I caught sight of Brandysnap's tail disappearing round a corner, and then Celandine let out a heart-rending neigh which drowned the singing birds and echoed in the hills.

She was sweating by the time we reached the small village of Cripton-under-Water, and I was so hot that I felt a swim in the little gurgling river would be welcome. In fact, I was looking dreamingly at the sun on the water when Celandine suddenly crossed the road and stood next to Brandysnap.

Harriet was talking enthusiastically to a fair-haired girl on a large roan hunter. "Yes, he's marvellous," she said. "I don't think I could have found a nicer pony if I had searched the whole world. He's wonderfully willing and so good in the stable to groom and that sort of thing."

"And is that your sister?" asked the fair-haired girl, looking at me, as I vainly struggled to make Celandine cross the road back to the river's side.

Harriet turned in her saddle and seeing me, said, "Gosh, no! I should hope not. We don't like each other at all, though we do go to the same school."

I felt a fool as I tried again to make Celandine leave Brandysnap and I felt furious. Then my parents arrived in the Land Rover and Mummy lent out of the window and said, "Hallo, Harriet! Andy, why must you go on pretending you two are arch enemies?" I realised we looked friends—with our two ponies standing so close together.

Harriet smiled at my parents and then she said to me, "Do get away, You give me claustrophobia."

"You don't own this side of the road," I muttered angrily. Then desperation made me hit Celandine with my hunting whip.

A woman said, "Oh, you cruel little girl! Fancy
143

hitting a poor dumb animal like that!" And Celandine leaped so far across the road that she nearly landed me in the river.

I looked around at the field. The Master had his big bay gelding out to-day: his wife, a hard-faced young woman, was mounting her dark-brown mare. Jon, Gillian and Susan were all present and about thirty other children, two of whom I knew vaguely.

My parents parked the Land Rover and came across to me. I was afraid they would bring up the subject of my broken friendship with Harriet, but they tactfully left it alone.

"Gingersnap looks a bit hot. Did you have to hurry over?" asked Daddy.

"Celandine, darling," corrected Mummy.

"No, but she was excited. She wouldn't walk a step. I couldn't calm her down," I told them.

"She must have known she was going hunting. It's funny how horses have these premonitions," said Daddy; and I felt as though I had told a lie.

Presently hounds moved off. It was a Children's Meet so there was no reason why I should not, as a child, be up in the front. I turned Celandine and, saying good-bye to my parents, I fell in behind Jon, who was directly behind the Master's wife.

A moment later, I felt a bang from a stirrup against my ankle, and looking round, saw Harriet was at my side.

I said, "Ow," and then I tried to get in front of Jon, so as to be away from Harriet, but Celandine was determined to stick with Brandysnap and there wasn't room amongst the crowd of jostling horses to have an argument. So Harriet and I rode side by side without looking at each other.

Susan was behind us on the ever-patient Nutmeg and, to my horror, she called, "I say, have you two made it up at last? . . . jolly good! I'm so glad . . . that's wizard." It was nice of her to care, I suppose, but so tactless at that moment.

Harriet and I both made another attempt to turn our ponies around and our ankles banged together.

Then the Master raised his hand and we all stopped in a narrow lane, while the huntsman rode on to put hounds into covert. There was a general whisper, because the Master had forgotten to deliver the traditional speech at the meet, and then there was a "Ssssshh!" from a grown-up at the back.

Presently the Master asked Jon to ride across a grass field and mark a point, and I prayed that he might not ask me to do anything, because I was afraid I would not be able to make Celandine leave Brandysnap.

We heard the huntsman encouraging his hounds and the blast of his horn; and then the Master led the way across two fields and we waited at the sire of a birch wood. Brandysnap and Celandine insisted on keeping together; and, as neither Harriet nor I wanted an open fight with our mounts in front of everyone, we could do nothing about it.

Celandine pulled a good deal with her head down and, to my consternation, I noticed a local equitation expert watching my frantic attemps to bring it up again. He was mounted on a superb light-weight hunter, which was beautifully balanced and schooled, and he had a wonderful seat on a horse.

He was known to be a very outspoken man and famous on the Continent. I knew his comments would be unfavourable.

Soon a hound gave tongue amongst the birches and we heard the huntsman's cheer; and then another hound gave tongue, and another, and then the pack was in full cry. Brandysnap and Celandine were both trembling with excitement. The sun lay sparkling on the birches and the grass. Blackbirds took wing from the trees and soared up into the azure sky. A crash of music broke through the soft stillness of the morning; a flash of lemon and white, black and tan met our excited eyes, as hounds streamed out of covert, and then, above it all, rang out the horn's gone-away.

The Master waited about ten seconds and then he led the way across the rolling meadow at a hand gallop. Harriet, Susan and I were just behind him, and his wife brought up the rear. He halted at a gate and, remembering Mummy's instructions, I leaped off to open it. The handle and latch were wired, and I had a struggle to untwist the wire. The Master told Harriet to hold Celandine, and with both hands free I managed. The whole field waited while I mounted, and then we all galloped round the edge of several acres of young wheat. I wanted to fall in behind Susan, but Celandine took charge and, flinging down her head, bumped past Nutmeg and the equitation expert's horse and landed me directly behind Brandysnap.

The Master, hearing me pushing by the other riders, turned in the saddle and called, " 'Ware wheat!"

Harriet said, "For goodness' sake keep in single file."

Ahead of us we could see, spread out like a Christmas card, the pack of hounds, the huntsman, and Jon looking very small on his hired pony. The whipper-in had just left the covert with a couple of stragglers. It was a poor day for scent, with the bright sunshine drying the ground and a light sharp breeze, but the hounds held the line.

At the corner of the wheat field there was a low bar of about two feet six, which the Master took in his stride. Brandysnap followed, jumping with a flourish and then stopped so suddenly, to see if

146

Celandine was following, that Harriet shot over his shoulders. She landed on her hands and, at the same moment, Celandine whisked me over the bar, so I landed just behind Harriet. The equitation expert came next, and when he was over he gave me a short talk.

"Your pony," he said, "should not be ridden in a pelham: it is the wrong bit for her. Whenever you pull on the reins you lower her head more and more. You would do much better in a snaffle and drop nose-band. Then, with some schooling, she would soon go very well. She is a nice pony. And your friend's little chestnut—he should not be in a pelham either. He is different from yours and above the bit, but he needs a snaffle, too."

We were all cantering across a field when this conversation took place. My eyes were on hounds, but I said, "Yes, I see. Thank you very much."

"You do not mind me telling you, do you? This is a children's day and the old who are out should help the young. It's a pity to see you at war with your pony," he continued.

"No, thank you very much," I said, and then Celandine finished the conversation by neighing wildly and swerving away to join Brandysnap.

We could still see hounds a field ahead of us and we could hear the horn cheering them on. The cold breeze was in our faces and stung our ears and made our eyes water. Clods of earth were flung up by the horses' hoofs and my face was soon splattered with mud.

We saw hounds enter a copse of firs, as we squeezed through a gap in a six-foot-high hedge. And then, by the sudden quietness, we knew they had lost the line.

Presently we pulled up a few yards from the copse and the Master said, "A little check. Some of your ponies have found that gallop hard going. Dismount, children, and rest them a little."

Celandine was certainly puffing and I dismounted, loosened her girth two holes and turned her head to the wind.

Steam rose from the hot horses and there was the smell of damp leather and warm wet ploughland. In the copse all was silent, except for the occasional crackle as a hound pushed through undergrowth. The huntsman sat still on his horse, trying to let hounds pick up the line themselves and trying to keep their heads down.

Brandysnap dragged Harriet in my direction until we were side by side. She tried to pull him away again, but the Master turned round and said, "Be quiet, please. Stand still. We don't want hounds' heads up." So there we were together again like two old friends, and our ponies were happy and contented.

CHAPTER EIGHT

WE LOST that fox for good, though how he eluded us nobody knows. We spent a little longer waiting outside the copse, and then the huntsman brought out hounds and cast them in the adjoining fields. There was a herd of bullocks, which the Master and whipper-in had to hold up in a corner, and they may have fouled the scent.

Presently we crossed the road, climbed a steep hill of scrub and brambles and cantered across a long stretch of ploughland to draw a few acres of well-kept woodland at the top.

To my horror, the Master turned to me and said, "Do you see that far corner where the gate and two tall firs are? Will you ride there and watch out? Keep your eyes skinned—you may see a fox."

"What did you say?" I asked in panic, unable to believe my ears, though I had heard perfectly well. He repeated his request slowly and patiently, and I felt stupid.

"Right. Yes. Thank you very much," I said, when he had finished, and then I urged Celandine into a canter and to my surprise she went without argument. But in a few seconds I was aware of galloping hoofs behind me and I heard the Master call. "All right, then —go with your friend. Yes, two pairs of eyes are better than one; but no talking." And a moment later Harriet was beside me.

"I couldn't stop Brandysnap," she gasped. "He wanted to be with Gingersnap."

"Celandine," I corrected. "Did you ask the Master if you could come?"

"No, I just cried out in despair, 'I'm going, too,' as I was borne away; and he thought the whole thing was intentional."

"Oh, I see," I said, remembering that Harriet had told Muriel in cold blood that I was a conceited pig.

We reached the dark firs, which were silhouetted dramatically against the clear shining sky.

We brought our ponies to a halt and looked over the gate down into the valley where the brown and green fields lay like patchwork in the sunshine and the cottages and farm buildings looked tiny, like toys. And the river was a broad band of shiny silver paper.

We did not speak to one another, but fastened our eyes on the edge of the wood and the long slope leading down to the sleepy valley. A little, light-hearted breeze stirred the leaves and tiny rustles in the wood's undergrowth broke into our day-dreams and reminded us of our responsibilities. Soon we heard the sound

149

of hound and horn coming nearer through the trees.

Now and then a hound gave tongue and birds left the covert. Our ponies fidgeted and Brandysnap pawed the ground impatiently.

The huntsman came within a few feet of us and then turned left-handed, and soon the pack was moving out of earshot.

We kept our post, still watching in silence for the fox, and the sun beat down on us, and we were too warm in our hunting kit.

Occasionally we heard the toot of the horn and the distant cry of hounds. At last I spoke. "Do you think we ought to move on?" I asked.

"I don't know—supposing we do and then the fox breaks just here? We'll feel awful," said Harriet, twiddling Brandysnap's plaited mane.

"We don't want to get left," I said.

We waited a little longer, listening intently, but only the faint mooing of cows in the valley and the rumble of a plane came to us.

"Look, suppose you wait here for a moment, marking the point, while I pop round the corner and see if I can see hounds?" I suggested.

"O.K." agreed Harriet. "But don't be long and mind you come back for me."

"Of course I will come back for you," I said indignantly, before remembering we were no longer friends.

But we had not reckoned with our ponies and I had only ridden a few yards when I heard Brandysnap galloping after me.

"Can't you make him wait?" I called in exasperation. "Ssssh! Don't shout. You'll get hounds' heads up," said Harriet.

"Hounds' heads up?" I mocked. "They're in the next county by now, I should think."

"I thought I heard the horn just now. It would be

150

dreadful if they were really close by and we never saw the fox leave. We would let them all down," said Harriet. "Will you go back and wait, please, and let me ride on. I simply can't stop Brandysnap."

"All right. Go ahead, then," I said.

It was only with great difficulty that I made Celandine go back to the gate and fir trees, and I grew very hot. Once there she would not stand still for a moment, but dug up the grass and neighed loudly enough to frighten any fox. Then suddenly she could bear it no longer. With a great bound she threw me forward in the saddle and I lost both stirrups, and then we were off round the edge of the wood at full gallop. I scratched my face on a low bough and lost my crash cap when my head hit a branch; and then I regained my stirrups and started to try and stop. But Celandine's head was down, and by the time I began to get her under control we had caught up with Harriet, who was trying to make a reluctant Brandysnap hurry.

"I'm as bad as you," I said. "I couldn't wait."

"Oh well, can't be helped. I don't believe there's a hound left in covert. They must have broken the far side and we never heard them. Look at these hoofmarks," said Harriet, fixing her eyes on the ground.

"We've probably missed the run of the season," I remarked dolefully.

"Pessimist!" cried Harriet. . . . It was getting like old times again. And then suddenly she seemed to remember again that I had proved a poor friend. "Look, let's part. It's silly to keep together. If we each go our separate ways, one of us is sure to find them."

I was disappointed, but I was determined not to show it. "All right," I said coldly. "Here we are at the head of two tracks—which one will you take?"

"Toss," she suggested. I spun a penny and she called "Heads," and won.

151

"You choose," I said; and again it was like old times when we were friends.

She took the sharp left track and I took the middle way, into a patch of scrub, which sloped steeply towards a village.

Celandine dodged the prickles and neighed hysterically, and I could hear Brandysnap answering. I wanted to listen for the sound of hound or horn, but the ponies made it impossible. I felt a faint sick feeling in the pit of my stomach. . . . I had missed a run. I was lost. . . . I would have to tell my parents all about it. I could hear, in my imagination, my mother's voice saying, "But didn't you hear them leave covert? Oh, Andy, you *must* have. Did you just stand there? On and on, like 'The boy stood on the burning deck'? Never mind, you'll have some more hunting next year. . . ." Next year! I thought. Months and months away—anything may have happened by then.

At that point my thoughts were interrupted by Harriet's voice. Clearly and rather shrilly, she called, "Andy, where are you? Andy, Andy! Come quickly."

Without another thought, I turned Celandine and galloped back the way I had come. I soon found Harriet, standing and holding a frantic Brandysnap.

"Oh, I'm so glad you've come! I couldn't do a thing with him after you left. He bucked and he plunged and he nearly lay down. Honestly, I thought he had gone crackers," she gasped.

"They are both crackers. They are crackers on each other," I said. "If we are ever going to find hounds we had better stay together."

"Yes, thank you," said Harriet, and then she gave one of her mother's sparkling smiles and mounted.

"I think hounds must have broken where they were put into covert," I said thoughtfully. "We couldn't have heard them then. It means the fox was running up-

152

wind, but I believe foxes do sometimes."

"That sounds very professional," said Harriet. "Come on then, let's get round the other side as fast as we can."

We galloped abreast down the broad track, with the thud of eight hoofs in our ears and the breeze refreshing our faces.

"That was wizard! Brandysnap is quite different when he is with Gingersnap," said Harriet, as we swung out into a field.

And then we saw hounds far down below, running towards the copse where we had lost our first fox, and only the huntsman was with them.

"There, there!" cried Harriet. "Aren't they wizard?"

"Running like smoke," I said. "A sheet would cover them."

"You and your hunting terms!" laughed Harriet.

We trotted down the long hill, which we had climbed so slowly an hour earlier.

And, as we reached the bottom, hounds swung left-handed, away from the copse and towards the shining river. We opened the gate for our ponies and crossed the narrow village road; then we rode at a low thorn hedge of about three feet, at which both our ponies refused.

"I've never jumped higher than two feet," said Harriet.

"It's silly to ride at it side by side. I'll lead the way," I suggested. I was determined to get over the hedge this time, and something of my feeling must have reached Celandine, because she jumped it beautifully, although I was riding her away from her friend. Brandysnap snatched at the reins and simply whisked Harriet over in pursuit of Celandine. The next moment we were galloping across a long stretch of grassland.

Now we heard the horn again and, more distant, the cry of the hounds. "Oh, it's wonderful! I shall never, never forget this day," called Harriet.

"Yes, it's super," I said, more soberly for I was looking for a gate or jumpable place out of the field.

"Head for the corner," I said at last. "There's a low rail there . . . the corner by the copse. I can't see another gate."

The breeze was on the left of us now and clouds were rising in the west to mar the beautiful clear blue of the sky; but sunlight still lay aslant the meadows and gilded the hedges and the tree-tops.

We jumped the rail in the Corner, and Harriet fell off head first in the plough, and I lost both stirrups.

Brandysnap stopped and stood by Celandine, and I took his reins. Harriet jumped to her feet and laughed. Her face was covered in plough and she spat out mouthfuls of earth before mounting again.

A spinney of firs hid hounds from us and we aimed at reaching the other side as soon as possible. We found a furrow and galloped across the long stretch of plough without tiring our ponies very much.

A low pheasant gate barred our entrance to the wood and, as the catch seemed difficult, we decided to jump it. This time it was I who fell off, but I managed to twist by body in mid-air so I landed on my feet.

"Bad luck!" called Harriet, "but you landed like a professional. Wish I could fall on my feet."

"I think we ought to give the ponies a short breather," I said. "I mean, they are not fit. It would be terrible if we damaged their winds."

Harriet agreed, so we led the ponies to the other side of the spinney, where a strong breeze was blowing up across the river, and tried to make them stand and rest. But now we could hear the horn and hounds quite plainly and the ponies were wildly excited.

Harriet fell off head first in the plough

Celandine trod on my left big toe twice, and Brandy-snap butted Harriet hard in the tummy three times, so, exasperated, we mounted again and cantered round the edge of the wheat field. Then, opening a gate, we entered a narrow muddy lane and saw a farm labourer just ahead of us. He wore very muddy breeches and gaiters and a leather jacket, and over his shoulder he carried a large sack.

Catching him up, I asked if he had seen hounds and he told us they had crossed the lane only five minutes before.

"Carry on down this lane till you come to an old cart-track on the left," he continued. "Then follow the track till you get to the stack of straw, where you'll find a gap into the beans. If you cut round the edge of them beans—don't go across them, mind, or Jack Wilkins *will* 'ave something to say to the hunt—and then you'll see a scrubby wood—Blackman's Patch, they callit— and that's where I reckon you'll find hounds."

We thanked him and cantered on down the lane. Soon we found the track and then we saw the straw stack, yellow in the sun, and heard the horn again. Each moment now we heard the cry of hounds more clearly; and our ponies needed no urging. Slowly we picked our way round the beans, while a glorious crash of music rang out across the countryside and was echoed, by the woods and hills.

We saw Blackman's Patch and amongst the scrub a flash of black and tan; and then we saw the huntsman's horse and a scarlet coat, bright against the dark background of the trees.

We brought our ponies to a standstill outside the wood and listened with care. Hounds had lost their fox, but every now and then they would give tongue for a few moments.

Presently we heard the huntsman call "Whoo-oop, wind 'im!" And then a long sad blast on the horn told us the fox had gone to earth.

We hesitated for a few moments, afraid we might be mistaken, but then the huntsman blew long and dolefully again.

"Let's ride in and see," I said.

In a corner of the little unattractive wood hounds were marking a great mound of sandy earth with a large entrance on the left side of it.

"Glad to see someone," said the huntsman. "Where's the rest of the field?"

"Gosh! We don't know," answered Harriet, dismounting to rest Brandysnap.

"Haven't seen them this last twenty minutes and I last saw Ted up on the Marksbury road. Gawd knows where he is now." The huntsman dismounted as he spoke and made a fuss of the young hounds. "We've had a good run and no mistake. What happened to you?" he asked.

We explained and he told us hounds had broken at the other end of the wood. "You couldn't have heard them—not where you were standing. But you shouldn't have hung on so long. Never let hounds get right out of earshot, and view," he finished.

Presently we left the wood feeling very superior as we jogged behind hounds. The huntsman told me to get a lemon and white dog hound out of a clump of undergrowth, and I rode back and cracked my whip and made what I hoped were the correct noises. He took no notice of me at all and I was just beginning to despair, when the huntsman blew the horn again and then he suddenly raised his old wise head and, after giving me a long contemptuous glance, left the wood.

I caught up with the pack, and Harriet was pointing down towards the river, where we could see the field riding in single file along a narrow track in the osier beds.

Clouds had blown up across the sky; the sun was hidden from sight, and down by the river, amongst the osiers, it looked damp and cheerless.

"Well they can't say I didn't blow often enough," said the huntsman. "Goodness knows how they lost us."

We rode down a long cart-track. The Master had seen us and was approaching at a canter, followed by nearly thirty children and five grown-ups. Their mounts were splattered with mud, but at the sight of hounds, became filled with new energy. Harriet and I felt smug as we rode behind hounds.

We turned and grinned at one another, and then I saw Susan, and Jon and Gillian waving to us and I waved back. I was glad hounds had not killed their fox. I was glad I had been asked to mark a point and, most of all, I was glad Harriet and I were friends again.

CHAPTER NINE

ALL TRACE of sunshine had left the cloudy skies when Harriet and I turned for home. The chilliness of a spring evening was already in the air although it was barely four o'clock. It seemed incredible that, but an hour before, this countryside of soft greens and greys and browns had been sparkling and bright in sunshine.

The ponies were anxious to be home, and walked briskly and happily side by side.

"We could not have kept up our quarrel much longer with Gingersnap—sorry, Celandine—and Brandysnap so devoted to each other," said Harriet, laughing.

"I think I'll drop the Celandine and let her be Gingersnap again," I said. "Would you like to put Brandysnap with her to-night? They've both been so lonely. But we must try and school them not to be so nappy when we are riding. It's awful if we can't be parted."

"Even the best of friends must part," quoted Harriet. "But you know the equitation expert who was out to-day? Well, he's taking the next Pony Club Rally and I vote we both go."

"That's a wizard idea! I bet we get terribly told off. But we'll learn an awful lot."

We rode on in silence and my thoughts drifted back to the end of the hunt. The Master had been very surprised to see us there with the huntsman and he had said some very encouraging things about our "riding across country," which I don't think I will repeat, because it might sound boastful. The equitation expert had been very nice too, and the other children had all been filled with curiosity to know how we had managed to find hounds again.

We had been allowed to act as whippers-in until Ted appeared on a borrowed horse and explained that his own mount had cut a knee on wire and was in a nearby farmyard.

Then we had bade everyone good night and took the narrow winding road home with our minds full of the day's happenings. Presently we talked of the hunt in detail, discussing each jump and fall over and over again, and then, suddenly, Harriet said:

"Did you really say I cadged rides on Peppermint and *always* left you all the grooming and tack-cleaning to do? And did you say I cheated at prep. and never helped Mummy with the washing up?"

She sounded so funny and so serious, and the questions seemed so ridiculous, that I began to laugh.

"I don't think it's very amusing," she said.

And then I remembered I had some questions to ask *her*. "Of course, I didn't say all that . . . *cheating at prep.* sounds like something out of a school story for girls," I said. "But, what about you telling everyone I was a conceited prig! But let's forget all that and have an armistice."

"I never said you were a conceited prig!" declared Harriet hotly. "I never said a thing against you—at least, hardly a thing—to anyone! Certainly nothing really spiteful. Who told you I had called you that?"

"Muriel."

"Well, it was a lie."

"She told me lots of other things besides. Did *she* tell you about the cheating?" I asked.

"Yes, and that you called me a false friend and a snooty bumptious spoilt child," said Harriet.

159

"You might have known that I never use the word snooty" I said reproachfully.

It dawned on us then that Muriel had behaved like the wicked girl in a school story. She had been jealous of our friendship and annoyed that I had left the gang, and she had purposely added fuel to the fire. It seemed incredible that we had not realised this earlier, that we had both been willing to believe her without hesitation.

"I never thought people like that really existed," said Harriet. "And we just lapped it up!"

We both began to giggle then.

"It all seems so idiotic now," I said. "And Daddy and Mummy said it was idiotic all along, but I wouldn't believe them. Won't the dogs be pleased?"

"We have the ponies to thank," said Harriet again. "They wouldn't allow us to be enemies."

"They are so happy to be together again now. I suppose we ought to give them a rest to-morrow, but what about going for a long, long ride the next day?" I suggested.

"Yes, we can take sandwiches and explore the Sparbury woods—you know, the haunted ones," said Harriet.

"And jump those broken-down steeplechase fences on the Fenwood gallop and find the old Roman Road," I continued.

Slowly the early evening mist came down from the hills and spread across the quiet meadows and hid the dark waters of the river from our sight. Softly then came the rain, falling in a gentle Scottish drizzle, blown by the western winds.

"It will probably be wet the day after to-morrow and our parents won't allow us to take sandwiches," I said.

"Pessimist!" cried Harriet.